WINTERFOLK

WINTERFOLK

JANEL KOLBY

HARPER TEEN
An Imprint of HarperCollinsPublishers

Library of Congress Control Number: 2017949566
ISBN 978-0-06-248700-1

Typography by Sarah Nichole Kaufman
17 18 19 20 21   PC/LSCH   10 9 8 7 6 5 4 3 2 1
❖
First Edition

To Bodi

PROLOGUE

I WASN'T ALWAYS A GHOST. I was told to be. Dad and King said it was for protection.

My protection. Their protection.

The Winterfolk's.

The problem with being a ghost—

Is that no one can see you.

1

SOMETIMES I'M A GHOST.

But this morning's air is heavy with the scent of our bodies, me and Dad's. Our unwashed laundry. Our rock dreams.

And I remember.

I'm not a ghost.

I'm real and I'm warm beneath my fleece blanket. A draft creeps up to my face, but I remember I have breath, and I blow. The draft escapes through the top of our vented tent with a sky window to my trees.

Seagulls call to each other from high—one after another—and gossip about the ocean. One tells a fairy tale about a girl who turned fifteen. She fell in love with a boy and left her world to find him.

It was never about the boy, I tell the bird.

The bird's voice dips behind the trees. The trees hide everything. His squawk blends in with the blur of trains, trucks, freeways, and planes to imitate the whoosh . . . whoosh . . . of the ocean, one wave never like the next.

I stretch out my legs, and my toes touch our full laundry bag. Beside it sags my faded blue duffel with clean clothes, and beside that is our box of food, which used to be for my shoes. My toes tip the box, and a lonely apple thuds to the side. Dad saved it for me. I should eat it, but my stomach is full of worms.

Not actual worms. I know that. I'm the one who's hungry.

But it's easier to believe the worms are responsible for the holes in my stomach. Worms get in everywhere, especially apples fallen from trees. It doesn't matter how far they've fallen. Rot begins as soon as they're detached, and the worms know where to find them.

I want my morning blackberries, still in season. I can pluck them straight from the bush and into my mouth. From one home to the next. No chance to rot. But I can't go alone. I need to wait for King.

I pull my book from under my pillow and check to see if Dad's asleep. He's on the other side of the tent, under his own blanket, his back to me. His silver hair glows green from the light through our tent, and the kit of shiny glass beads props his head. An empty wine bottle has toppled his stack of finished bracelets.

My fingers rest on the solid cover of my book.

I don't need to see the words to know what it reads. *Fairy Tales.* My long, pointed fingernails ache to trace the words to make them real, and I let them. Trace one letter after another as if I can write.

Fairy Tales.

The girl on the cover doesn't know what a fairy tale is. No one dared tell her.

I touch the mermaid's hair, brown-black like mine. It floats around her head when she's under the water. Everything is different under the water, but that doesn't make it less real. Seashell armor covers her chest, and her scales reach down from her waist.

I open to the first page, strong as cloth from all my reading.

The story begins in the deep, deep ocean.

But that's not the story I read.

"Beneath these stars, no man can judge another. And that's where we live, baby. What palace is grander than that? See that one? The biggest and the brightest? That one's always true. We're all the same in her light, and it's because of her I met your momma. I wished for her. How many people do you think have wished on that star?"

I'm ten years old.

I adjust myself on the flatter part of the rock and try to ignore my stomach. "I dunno. Twenty or thirty?"

He scoots himself over to give me more room.

"In all our lifetimes? As long as humans have lived on this planet? Everyone in the world can see her at one point or another. Come on, baby, you can do better than that."

I look at the shimmer-stars above us and the honey-drip moon. "Too many to count."

"That's right." He tilts the bottle and drains it with a last swallow, and wipes his mouth with the back of his hand. "Too many to count." He examines the empty bottle. "And gone too soon. Not everyone gets their wish."

I stare at Momma's star. "She's getting heavy, isn't she? With all those wishes on her. She's gonna fall. Maybe she wants to."

"Nah. It's all those frivolous wishes hanging on her that might cause an accident. All those ex-pec-ta-tions. Stars don't want to fall, but they do. Most of them burn up in the atmosphere, but not all of them. It's the wish. The wish that matters. If it's really special, that star'll cool down. Turn to a rock. To protect the wish."

That star is sagging. I can see it. And it's partly because of me.

He shakes his bottle. "You know what this cost me? One bracelet. That's one hundred and—"

"Twenty-five beads. Will you teach me tomorrow? I sorted the beads like you said."

"You wished on that star, didn't you? Wished that I'd teach you?"

I hang my head. It's hard to keep the wishes pent up inside.

"Causing that star all kinds of trouble. You know I can't, baby."

"But you said—"

"Not yet. When I get asked at the market, *did you make these*, I want to reply with honesty, *yes, I did, with these hands alone*. Eyebrows would sure raise if I told them they were made by my baby girl."

"Why?"

"They'd want to know where you are, and then they'd take you from me. We've got to stick together. There's nothing out there worth losing what we have here. Believe me. You've got to be my little ghost for now. It's just us two. Your momma would want that. I'll teach you someday. Maybe next year. Don't get ahead of yourself, and don't go wishing. She wouldn't want any of those stars to fall. You know that. She took good care of them—"

The back of my heels hit the rock. "She'd want me to hide?"

"Who's hiding? We live under the stars. They keep watch on us, and we keep watch on them. Look at that sad star now. You've got to be more careful with your wishing."

That star does look sad. I should keep to collecting instead of wishing. "How can I fix it?"

"Close your eyes," he says. "Close your eyes and take back your wish."

I close my eyes and take it back, along with the one about

a double scoop of ice cream over a banana split.

"That's right," he says. "Now look at that sky. Doesn't she look brighter?"

My stomach feels empty. "I don't feel good."

"Just look up, babe. Up there is your medicine. *Star medicine*. You gave her some of what she needs, and she'll give some to you. Watch how she shines down on you."

I tilt my head back and let her shine.

"You've got to respect the wishes that have gone before you. They've got to have their turn, too. How many stars do you think are up there?"

I look back at the sky. "Too many to count."

"That's right. Too many and too few." He knocks the empty bottle against his knee. "Yours is up there to use one day. Do you see it? Do you see your star?"

"No, Daddy."

"Keep looking. It's up there. But careful not to wish."

Three scratches on the tent make me shut the book.

Three.

King.

I stuff the book back under my pillow and scratch the tent back. The weather's not cold enough for me to cover my tank, but I pull on sweatpants and twist my hair into a stocking cap. Last, my boots, before unzipping the door.

Yellow light comes in, along with a snap of fresh air.

King's head is turned—always surveying—not looking at

me. Behind him is his tent. Steps away. Never too far. Black and blue shadows tangle his hair over the sleeves of a fresh, black T-shirt. He brushes his hair from his warm-penny face, tinged with pink. I want to hug him as I used to.

"You were with the sun all day yesterday," I say. "She kissed your cheeks."

He smiles. "I stayed as long as she cared to watch."

"And then you went out with the moon. I heard your tent zip up. You came back late."

"You shouldn't wait for me."

Of course he doesn't want me to wait. He's only two years older, but I'm not as strong as the sun. Or as luminescent as the moon.

"Someday," I say.

The pink of his cheeks gets pinker. But I'm not the one doing it to him. He's looking at whatever he did yesterday without me. And all the yesterdays.

"Maybe the sun didn't kiss you," I say. "Maybe she slapped you."

His smile falls. "What d'you know about that?" He looks into the tent, which is absurd. Dad only sees the stars.

I push King's shoulder, and his eyes come back to warn me. "Only fairy tales," I tell him.

"Fairy tales?"

"Sometimes there's a kiss, and then a slap." I clap my hands once, and the sound scares some birds. Their wings flap up from a tree.

King puts his finger to his lips. "Don't do that. You're gonna wake him."

Yes, that's right. Don't make a sound. Plus, if Dad wakes, King would have to say *morning*, since he promised he would try to get along.

I shake my head. Not to worry. From the looks of that bottle, Dad will sleep as deep and long as the ocean.

"Did you bring me another book?" I ask.

"Ready to return that one?"

"No."

"Then, no book. Berries?"

My stomach answers.

King steps back when I climb from the tent and knocks over my black-white speckled rock, as oval as an egg.

"Careful," I say.

He sets it proper in my rock path of wishes, almost fifteen rocks wide. The path winds in a circle 'round the tent—two more needed to complete the fifteenth row. Almost fifteen years. Where you start is where you end.

He pats the rock firm. "There, now. No harm'll come to her."

I kneel to check for cracks where any dreams could leak. She seems to be intact.

I look up to my trees, my Bruces and Evergreens. "You take care of her," I tell them, and one Bruce nods. The books call them spruce, but I call them Bruce. Evergreen can keep its name, since she's so true. Bruce is a man, of course, and

Evergreen is a woman. Beyond them are more Bruces and more Evergreens. Bruce, Evergreen, Bruce, Evergreen, Bruce, Bruce, Evergreen, Evergreen. All my soldiers. Standing by. Clumps of bushes fill their spaces. Green to hide our green tents.

King picks up a dead stick and taps it hard against his thigh.

Brittle bones, brittle bones. All too easily snapped.

He lets go. Surprised. And throws the broken stick aside.

"You ready?" he asks.

I stand.

He tosses a bottle of water to me, and I look to our empty rain catch—tarp open wide with a gutter that leads to a bucket. I guzzle the bottled water and enjoy the drips that run from the corners of my mouth. My stomach expands to accept it.

I am the rain.

He takes the empty bottle and throws it inside his tent.

"You have more? For when he wakes?" I don't like to ask, and he knows.

He shrugs. Unspoken. It's available for me to take, like anything else he has.

"Come on," he says.

Branches crackle beneath his boots, but not beneath mine. Ghosts don't make a sound. King got me these boots from the salivating army. My feet slip around, and the cold gets trapped in the extra space at my toes.

A flash of red appears below. The Lady. Wandering the way she does in her red dress and brown hair hanging loose. Of all the Winterfolk, she's been here the longest, but she's not the oldest. As old as Dad, maybe.

"She's following," I say.

King looks behind. He goes to tug at his sleeve cuffs but remembers he's in a T-shirt and rubs his wrists instead. His mind is uncomfortable. "You been talking?"

The last of the red disappears. "Not since last winter."

A single drum plays down below—Hamlet's—a deep pulse in the hill only Winterfolk hear. I can almost smell the oatmeal, and I don't miss it.

"Breakfast," I say.

King touches a yellow-tinged leaf—the turning color, our warning sign.

Once the leaves turn, the rains will come with all their sliding. We'll move our tents down on the flatter part with the others, some without the daily sort of rules that keep their space clean. Not all the oatmeal in the world can hide it.

I rub my nose. "Winter should smell like candy canes. Remember that one I got for Christmas? I slept with it under my nose to smell at night. Had it for three days, then woke with it gone. Thought someone took it, but my tongue caught something sweet stuck in my back tooth. I'd eaten it in my sleep."

I suck at my teeth, and my stomach growls.

King picks the turning leaf from the tree and walks again.

"I heard there's a chocolate factory supposed to be built down the hill in one of them old breweries, pumping chocolate in the air twenty-four-seven. Think of smelling that. Be like eating chocolate all day."

Smelling's not eating, but he knows that.

"I hope it at least snows," I say. "Cover everything. Make it pretty. How those flakes float down to rest and turn into one big blanket. Ever wonder what it's like? To sleep like snow? Nearly still forever. I'd sleep on top if I wouldn't freeze. Better than any type of mattress I imagine. Do you think I'd disappear like the snowflakes?"

King tears the leaf in half and drops it. "Guess so."

"Guess so? You should know. You're the one who sells mattresses."

"I don't sell mattresses. I only swing the signs."

"You dance the signs."

He pauses and lowers his eyes. I know I've hit a nerve. "That's not dancing. I'm done with it."

"What do you mean?"

"The money's not worth it."

"But it's money. I could take your place."

His shoulders push forward. "Girls swinging signs . . . I haven't seen any. Maybe cuz they'd cause traffic accidents no matter what they look like. Girls like that—they belong in clubs. And that's not you."

"You did it."

His eyes dart to me, and my legs go numb. I finger the

gold-beaded necklace around my neck with the glued-shut locket.

A plane roars above, and he looks up to watch it pass. He breathes deep and pulls back his hair, as glossy as a crow's, into a neat ponytail with a band from his wrist. His eyes are soft when they come back to me.

"Rain," he says.

It isn't kind to remind someone about their past. Which is why we won't talk about dancing, his needles, or what happened days and nights and days ago. Why King goes with me to get the berries. And why we both won't think about it.

"Don't worry 'bout money," he says. "I'll figure something. Let's get your berries."

I nod and follow.

The worms in my stomach come alive as we reach the thorny blackberry bushes, bigger than the both of us. I don't hear the drum anymore. Just my stomach.

King puts a hand in his pocket, where I know there's a silver blade as long as my middle finger.

I reach out to the wild berries, and the thorns move aside. I pluck a plump berry that's loose from its stem and pop it in my mouth. I let it settle on my tongue first. Hardly nothing's better than a mouth that's full. Then I bite—just a little—and the sweet juice trickles to fill the empty spaces. And it's even better. Only liquid can fill empty spaces. Maybe ghosts. *Too many empty spaces*, Dad says before his wine. But I have my berries. And King.

My stomach urges me to pluck another. I won't argue with it.

"Aren't you gonna eat?" I ask King.

He shrugs. The bush has plenty but not as much as yesterday, and not as much as the day before.

I pluck another and hold it out to him. "Eat."

He can't deny me. His two fingers wrap from top to bottom while mine wrap side to side. A whole berry world in our fingers. He pulses his fingers—dares us to squish the great beauty. But he only teases.

I let go, and he scoops the little world in his mouth.

"Ripe." He wipes his mouth. He doesn't like stains.

"So, what're you going to do today if you're not working?" I ask.

He smiles.

Stay with me. I don't want to be alone.

A snap beyond the blackberry bush turns both our heads, and he goes for his knife. He jumps through the thick bush, and it snags at him as he tears through. My breath goes with him.

But the rest of me can't.

Not across those bushes. And never outside the Jungle.

I can't breathe.

The trees blur around me. Their leaves cover my ears and shut my eyes. I'm all blackness. They tell me to run. Can't stay here. They'll help me to run.

And I know they're right. They've seen what can happen.

I hold to one tree trunk as another reaches. Grips of rough bark. One to another. I feel for their ridges as they feel for me. And I run. Keep running.

Not sure how far I've come.

Keep running.

I will as long as they're with me.

My hand reaches to the next but slips off a smooth surface, and I stumble to my knees.

The tree didn't catch me.

"Rain!" King calls from somewhere behind.

I'm safe. That's why the tree didn't catch. King is coming, and he's bringing my breath. It comes back extra hard as I check my knees. But they're fine, and I breathe easier. Dad always says how I need to be more careful. Mending is hard to come by.

The tree shudders above.

I look up and teeter.

Now I understand why the tree didn't catch. Why it couldn't.

A bright yellow paper is stapled to it. Four staples. One on each side.

I reach to touch when all the trees call to me.

Look at me. Look at me.

My legs stand me up. Yellow papers. Yellow papers. On all the big trees around us. They'd be pretty decorations if they didn't have staples.

"Rain!"

My legs are heavy as I step to the tree that didn't catch me. I read.

CITY OF SEATTLE

PUBLIC NOTICE OF DEMOLITION

THIS PROPERTY IS OWNED BY THE CITY OF SEATTLE. IT IS UNLAWFUL FOR ANY PERSON TO ENTER OR OCCUPY THE AREA FOR ANY REASON. ANY UNAUTHORIZED PERSON FOUND ON THIS PROPERTY ON OR AFTER THE DEMOLITION DATE WILL BE FORCIBLY REMOVED AND PROSECUTED.

DEMOLITION DATE: OCTOBER 1

PLEASE VACATE THE PREMISES BY: SEPTEMBER 30

THE CITY OF SEATTLE WILL NOT TAKE RESPONSIBILITY FOR ANY DAMAGE OR THEFT OF PERSONAL BELONGINGS.

I read again and try to make sense.

The trees bristle behind me. King's here. He'll erupt if he sees. I cover the notice with my hands, though it won't be much use. If I were ivy, I could cover the papers on every tree.

My arms shake.

A tree taps my arm.

King taps my arm.

"Why'd you run?"

He's focused on my face. He doesn't yet see the trees.

His arms are full of wild bush cuts and scrapes, and a line of blood stretches down his cheek.

"I told you." He smears the blood. "Never run. Never, *ever* run. I'll take care of it—just like before. What if someone else found you? It wasn't even nothing. Just a squirrel."

"A squirrel," I say.

"A squirrel." He breathes hard. "Was lookin' out for us."

Of course. Of course he was. "Of course," I say.

He tilts his head at me. Then his eyes wander to my outstretched arms. Then out to all the trees.

"Are you okay?" I ask.

"What is this?" he says.

"A story."

King's eyes harden. "About what?"

"A fairy tale, you wouldn't like it, because you only like real things. I'm tired." I yawn. And then I yawn for real cuz all I wanna do is curl up in my tent and pretend I never saw this. All the note means is that if you don't belong, get out. Maybe they heard what happened to me. Doesn't mean the folk who live here. "Let's go back. You can go on ahead. I'll be there in a minute." I yawn again, cuz now I can't stop and my eyes are tearing.

But he's already at one of the trees. He braces against it as he reads.

He's quiet.

I take cover behind my tree. Sit and plant my fingers in the earth.

"Fucking cowards. *Unauthorized person.* Why don't they just say what they mean? *Take your crap and get out.*"

I dig the toes of my boots in the dry earth. Searching for the bottom. Hasn't rained in days.

He rips the paper from the tree, and the tree grazes his knuckles. "Sanitation problem. That's what we are."

I look at my buried hands and feet. "They don't see us."

"Exactly." He tugs at his hair, and it comes loose from the elastic. "You see? Didn't even bother to spread the notices. Dumped them all here. We need to get out. There's too many of us now. Too much garbage." He begins to pace. "I've done this before. We'll find a place. Maybe south."

"You want us to leave?"

"Don't worry about your dad—I'll wave a bottle. I need to tell the Winterfolk."

I lift my hands from the dirt, and they look like they're part of the earth. He's right. How would they ever see us?

My toe hits a rock, and I pry at it with my foot. I pick it up and brush off the dirt—gray, blue, black. Used to be someone's wish. I'm sure of it, but might have been buried too long.

I put the rock to my ear.

Silence.

It happens to the best of wishes.

2

I FOLLOW HIM DOWN the hill. He rubs his knuckles, red and scratched. But he's not doing it to soothe. He's putting his hands back together. He's good at that. Must hurt, cuz trees are strong. But he doesn't let the pain reach his head. Can't be real if you don't feel it. I'm sure the tree felt it. The tree was right to fight back after he tore off that paper.

I brush my hand along the trunks as we pass. He didn't mean to hurt them. They know that. He'd do anything to protect.

I hold the rock to my chest. "They won't hurt the trees, will they?"

"Why not? Best way to get out rats, don't you think?"

"They can't do that," I say.

He laughs.

And he laughs.

But I don't let it reach my head. And I don't feel it.

We're going down, down. Past our camp, and down. He's going to tell them. The Winterfolk.

Bits of electric blue appear through the branches. A circle of twelve tents and a fire pit in the middle with the last of the morning's embers. Beside the pit, the oatmeal pot is already clean. A laundry line sags across two of the tents—with still-dirty jeans, boxer underwear, and a long floral skirt that used to have color. They wash their laundry in a bucket with a bar of soap. I've watched them. The water gets dirty fast with one bucket of water to share, and not everything gets clean. They share everything. I'm lucky with King, who finds our own way of cleaning.

Plastic buckets of potted flowers grace the entrances of tents, and wind chimes dangle from tent poles.

King won't let us have chimes. Too much noise.

"Stay here with the trees," he says.

He doesn't need to tell me.

Sabbath barks to greet King as he approaches. Big dog, a sheen of black fur. Matches King.

King strokes the top of Sabbath's head and behind his ears. He sits in the biggest chair and scoots it back, away from the pit. Heck comes out from his tent with a mug of coffee and a cigarette. As young as King but with rough skin and a webbed tattoo down his neck. There's a scar caught in there.

I know. I've seen how it waits to be eaten.

He shakes his head at his dog, who rests his head on King's feet. "Amigo?"

The dog ignores him.

I wonder if Sabbath will go with us when we leave.

Heck sits in a chair and sticks the cigarette in his mouth before clasping hands with King. He holds up his mug, and King waves it off. Heck looks tough, but I've seen how he gives the best of his plate to Sabbath.

Gray Hamlet comes next. Gray hair, gray skin, gray clothes. Cuz he's so giant. Have to fade out when you're that giant. Has wrinkles on his face for hiding the pieces of him that don't want to fade. We all have some of those pieces.

I look for his white bucket—not the one he uses for a stool, but the one that's a home for his twelve hamsters. Must be inside his tent. King says they dance—how Hamlet gets his pay—but I've never seen it. I wish he had his bucket. Haven't seen those hamsters in forever.

Hamlet sits on the other side of King. They don't clasp hands, but King nods with respect.

Couple more come out, young and old, but none as young as me. I am the youngest. Was always the youngest. That's what King said.

Some heads poke out of other tents. All pretend not to see me.

Like they do the Lady. On the other side of the camp. She sits and spreads her dress upon the ground. Her hair is different shades of brown, like the bark of a tree.

She sees me. And I see her.

King takes the note from his pocket, and the Lady turns her attention to him.

Can't hear what he says when he passes it around, but backs that were slumped now straighten. More come out of tents.

Heck reads the note while other hands tug at it. He lets go, and the chair falls as he stands. Sabbath lifts his head and whimpers.

King says something to Heck, and they stare at each other.

Hamlet doesn't read the note. Must already know what it says. He gets up and goes back into his tent.

Another crumples the paper and throws it in the pit.

The wind chimes clink like tin.

And one of them. A woman. She wipes at her face.

I know what that means.

But she shouldn't cry. No need to cry.

And then I'm there with her. Don't know how. But I hold her hand.

King tries to push me back.

The woman's eyes grow wide as if she's never seen me.

"We've just gotta stay invisible," I tell her. "We know how to do that."

She squeezes my hand tight.

I try to pull my hand away, but it hurts, and King yanks it from her.

"That's right." She rubs her face and stands.

And then she doesn't see me no more. Not without holding my hand. I almost give it back to her.

She wrings her skirt. "I didn't look at her."

The cold puckers the skin on my arm into raised pieces. I try to smooth it out with my rock.

The Lady stands.

Yes. She sees me.

I wave.

King looks off into the forest where I was looking, and frowns. Rubs his wrists.

"When you leaving?" Heck asks King.

"Huh?" King comes back to us.

"Your farewell?"

"Tomorrow," King says. "Change your mind."

"Nah," Heck says. "I'm staying, holmes. Your girl is right. About being invisible."

I almost want to hug him for acknowledging me.

"We'll stay long as we can," Heck says. "Then hide out while they clean this shit up—like how they clear the campers on Airport Way when the president's in town. Right? They don't wanna see what they don't wanna see, and it takes money to prosecute. You think they wanna spend it on us when they could use it for a new basketball stadium? I'll even thank them for takin' out my garbage. Leave 'em nice presents."

"I'm not worried about you." King lowers his voice.

"But . . . the others."

Heck takes a drag on his cigarette. Careful not to look at me. "You do what you gotta. I do my own."

King looks around, but no one looks back. "Don't do this."

Heck shrugs with the cigarette in his lips. "It's my home."

I climb up the hill after King. "You're worried about the Winterfolk. Why? They make themselves invisible. Same as us. What can happen?"

"Anything." He walks fast.

"What does that mean?"

"Means *anything*."

He brushes the leaves from his arms. My arms tighten and I want to push him. "Hey."

He stops and turns around. Shoves his hands in his pockets.

I squeeze the rock—for some of its wish to strengthen me. "I want to stay, too."

"Stay?"

"Yeah. I'll hide."

"In the trees?" he asks.

I nod.

"And where you gonna hide when there aren't any trees? *Demolished.* That's what the sign said. Everything gone. You think you're that invisible? You're not. Did you forget about the berries?"

I glare at him. It's not nice to talk about the past.

He swallows. "You don't get it. We're *not* real to them. We're either invisible—or we're rats. And when there are no more hiding places, the Winterfolk will need to run—that is, if they care enough. And then they're as good as rats running from BB guns. If they get away and split up—how many you think'll come back? Like Rosemary?"

I pull a lock of hair from beneath my hat. Rosemary was the only one who'd visit me. She used to weave my hair in a long braid down my back. Until King went to talk to her. He said we needed to be cautious. Better not to make friends.

They found her frozen under a bridge.

He grinds his foot on a tree root. A tree root getting squished. "I didn't tell her to leave."

"I know you didn't." I nudge his foot off the root with my own. "But it's coming on winter. How're they gonna make it without each other? Without you?"

"The Winterfolk will do their own, and we do ours. This is my decision."

"Why? Because you're older? I'm fifteen tomorrow, but you'll always be older, won't you? When will I get a say? And stop telling them they can't look at me—was fine when I was little, but now it's embarrassing. Like I'm any different from them."

"You *are* different."

I shake my head. "You've always worried about the bad—that it'll make me like them—but it's too late. I already know what bad is."

He points at my heart. "You've met it, but you haven't become it, and you never will. Plus, I haven't been telling them not to look. They're used to it."

"Is that how it started with the Lady? They got used to not looking?"

His face falls. "Rain. You know she's not real. Right?"

"No, I know. That's what happens when no one looks at you. You want me invisible forever."

He clenches his teeth and gets walking again.

I can't talk to him.

The door of our tent hangs open. Dad is awake.

"Rain?" Dad calls.

I follow King to his tent, and he gets me some water.

Dad coughs. I set the new rock in my path—almost fifteen full circles wide—and take off my shoes before I climb in.

He stretches in his sleeping bag, and I hand him the plastic bottle.

Dad takes a sip. "Why were you gone so long?"

"Wasn't long. Got berries."

He nods. Takes another sip. Looks at his watch.

"King go with you?"

"Um-hmmm. Got scared by a squirrel." I fold my blanket in a square. Put it on my pillow. Roll up my sleeping bag and take out the hand sweeper.

Brush brush. Brush brush. Across the floor of the tent.

Tiny bits of earth that've lost their way. A small ant. I scoop him up and out the door.

I wait for Dad to get out of his bag. Then I wait for him to put on his shoes and go out the same way. Bits of earth. Bits of earth.

When he's gone, I fold up his blanket and roll his bag.

Brush brush. Brush brush.

I put the empty bottles—one glass, one plastic—into a bag and set it outside the door for King. Then carefully put the finished bracelets into Dad's backpack for the market.

I roll the sleeping bags back out and fold them in half. Cushions for sitting.

I wait for Dad.

Wonder if King'll talk with him about the paper on the trees.

Dad takes off his shoes before he comes back in.

Looks nice. Is what he says every day. But today. He doesn't say anything.

King talked.

He sits on his sleeping bag and stares at his stockinged feet.

"Tired," he says. "Aren't you tired?" He looks up at me.

I shake my head.

"Don't know if I'm up for walking," he says.

"You're not going to Pike Place? What about the bracelets?" And food. All we have is that apple.

"Pike Place?" he asks.

Oh. He's not talking about Pike Place.

I touch his hand, and he startles.

"Daddy—"

"You should learn the bracelets."

I put my hands in my lap. "Tonight?"

"Tomorrow."

"For my birthday?"

He looks to me. Figures me. Thirteen? Fourteen? Fifteen? Not sixteen. Can't be sixteen.

"So grown," he says. "I don't have anything to give you." His eyes go watery. They go extra watery the day after a full bottle. "Your mom would've—"

"The beads," I interrupt. "I've always wanted to learn."

He sniffs and nods. "Did you see the designs from yesterday?"

I forgot to look, but I climb over to hug him anyway. "Beautiful."

He pats my back. "They'll sell nice. Reminds me." He lets go and reaches for his kit. "Got another bag for you."

"Oh. Great."

He lifts the tray at the top and pulls out a bag the size of four empty sandwich ones. The bag is filled to the top with mixed colored beads. He gets them cheap when they're mixed. He sweeps them off a store floor. A trade. Must've taken weeks.

"Should take you some time to sort," he says. "Occupy your mind. Sound fun?"

I take the bag and smile.

His smile falters. "You used to beg to help me sort. But I'll teach you the beading tomorrow. You need to learn before you go."

I drop the bag. "Before I go?"

"Before *we* go. We've always been fine, haven't we? And this time King will be with you. He knows his way. Always finds a way. Smart kid. Remember when he found us on the corner? You were . . ." His mouth trembles. "You were ten."

"Dad—"

"This has been a good home to us. He's a good friend. Remember that. Never wanted us to separate. He knew we'd be better off here. And we have been. He kept up your reading. I wish you'd let him teach you how to write. You should know how to write. Never heard of reading without writing."

"Dad, why are you—"

He tilts his head. "Listen."

I listen.

"Is it raining? Your mother loved to hear the rain."

I've been running my hands through the beads. "No, Dad. It's just this." I pick up a handful and let them trickle between my fingers.

"Ah," he says. "I thought it was the rain. Then again, I imagine lots of things. You do, too, don't you?"

"I guess."

Three scratches on the tent.

Three.

"Mister," King says from outside. "I'm going to the outlet. Want to come with?"

Dad looks at me. "Do we need bread?"

"Yes."

King knows Dad sold bracelets yesterday. Best to change the money to food now before he trades the rest with Winterfolk for drink.

Dad smiles. "I'll get groceries. How about that? You'll have some good food for your birthday. Tomato soup, maybe. Heated. With bread and cheese. And you can work on the beads while we're gone."

"Sounds nice."

King holds the door flap as Dad climbs out, and my eyes sting.

King pokes in his head. "You okay in there?"

I want to tell him again how I don't want to leave, but I know he won't listen to me.

I hold up the bag of beads. "Just fine."

He tucks imaginary strands of fallen hair behind his ear. It's what he can't see that bothers him most. "We'll talk when I'm back, okay?"

I get out the tray, separated by compartments, and drop a cornflower-blue bead in an empty square. "Sure."

When he's gone, I put the tray aside. Unfold my sleeping bag and lie down.

I slip my hand beneath my pillow and grasp my *Fairy Tales*

book with the girl on the cover.

I pull the knit cap off my head and spread out my hair. I'd rather be a mermaid than a ghost.

I take out the book and stroke the mermaid's hair. Long and smooth. Rising in the water.

Mom's hair was like hers. I remember.

The water. The water.

Mom used to sing about the water.

And she'd hum in a way she said dolphins could hear.

An airplane flies across the sky window.

I see them, but they don't see me.

3

"RAIN?" KING'S SHADOW APPEARS in the dark of night from the lantern glow on the other side of the tent.

I thought they'd be back sooner. Been hours since I sorted the bag. Read my book twice. Cleaned the tent again.

"I have some food," he says.

My stomach growls. I didn't eat the apple.

He unzips the tent and pokes his head in. "Rain?"

I roll across my sleeping bag. Turn my back to him.

The tent brightens as he climbs in. I hear him zip the tent behind. A paper bag crinkles when he sets it down.

"There's bread and nacho dip in here," he says. "Are you hungry?"

I pull my stocking cap over my ears.

He sets the lantern closer, then sits down on Dad's sleeping bag behind me. "He's with the Winterfolk. Saying bye, I guess."

I'm sure he'll be saying it till morning. I don't mind. They're his friends. Got to say good-bye to friends. After I cleaned the tent, I sat with my own friends.

I couldn't tell them good-bye.

But they knew. Branch touched branch to spread the news. They'd heard everything.

Demolished. That's what King said.

I watched the darkness spread across their leaves, and they whispered to me.

We'll still have our roots. We'll stretch them across the earth to find you.

King talks to my back. "Are you scared about leaving tomorrow?"

I tuck my hands under my pillow and hold on to my book. "The sign said leave by the thirtieth. We still have a full day before then. Why leave tomorrow?"

I need more time. To figure things out.

"Why *not*?" he says. "No point in staying."

"No point in leaving."

He puts his hand on my shoulder, and his warmth seeps all the way through me. Was it always this warm? "You don't gotta be scared," he says. "I know it's long since you've been out. Too long, probably. But there's nothing to worry."

"I'm not ready to leave," I say.

His fingers tighten on my shoulder, and I turn onto my back to look at him.

He scoots his knees up and rests his arms on top of them. "Naturally. Been five years. Long enough to forget what it's like outside here."

"I don't think I'd know it."

"You'll know it again. And once we find a place, we'll set up your tent. Won't be any different."

I draw up my knees and lean them against his. There's that warmth again. "What would happen, you think, if they saw us? The city, I mean. If they really saw us. You think we could stay?"

King picks at a hole in his jeans forming on his knee. "See how I pay attention to this?" he says. "It only makes it worse."

Another type of hole rips my stomach. "It's too fast. I can't leave knowing I can't come back."

His eyes tell me he's weighing the thoughts that trip through his mind. He's seeing me in those thoughts. All those possibilities.

"You wanna try it out first?" he asks. "Like practice?"

"You mean you'd take me to the city tomorrow? And come back? I can have tomorrow?"

"Can't give you what's already yours. It *is* your birthday."

I almost forgot. The hole in my stomach gets smaller, and I hug my arms across me.

"Now, I know you've got that book under there," he says. "Wanna read to me?"

I take the book out while he settles on the sleeping bag, and I turn to my favorite story.

4

THE WIND CARRIES SPIRITS of brine and seaweed, and I lick my arm below my shoulder to taste the salt.

Maybe today I'll see the ocean.

The morning drum plays far and faint. My heart joins the drum and makes it louder. I open my eyes to the sunlight above. King should be here soon. *When you hear Hamlet's drum.* That's what he said.

I stretch my toes to the laundry bag at my feet. Extra full.

Dad's watch ticks slower than the drum, counting one second to the next, never wanting to jump ahead to see what might come. He breathes in deep, but I know he's not asleep. I know his eyes are just as open as mine to the new day.

The drum music stops.

Scratches outside the tent. Three. I jump to my knees.

King.

"You ready?"

I've been waiting.

I twist my hair up and pull on my stocking cap.

I unzip the door.

He turns his head to me, and my mouth tingles. I want to smile, because he's in his black velvet blazer, hair tied back. But nothing about his extra-fine face is smiling.

I nod to let him know I understand. We're not playing.

But he tugs the cuff of his sleeve, and I must smile.

Cuz he's King.

"Do I look fifteen?"

He almost smiles back. He holds out a green rock, marbled in pink.

"My birthday present?" I take the rock and hold it to my ear.

Whispers.

"Do you like it?" he asks.

I kiss it. "Will you place it for me?"

I hand it to him, and he steps back to put it in the final spot of my fifteen-stones-wide path.

His eyes get serious again. He comes back and holds out his hand to help.

"One minute," I say.

I crawl over my crumpled blanket and lean to Dad. Careful not to crush him.

His eyes close, and his cold ear numbs my lips.

"I'm going now. You'll teach me the beads? Tonight, like you said?"

He pulls his blanket up over his shoulders and tucks in his hands.

I wait for him. I don't expect him to agree, and I don't expect a *Happy Birthday*, but I do expect—

He nods his head. Just the down part, not the down and up. It could've been his head dropping as he falls back to sleep.

I pull his gray sweatshirt from our laundry bag and put it on over my tank top. The sweatshirt's so big it falls to my knees like a dress would, but it has a pouch in front to collect things. I would wear my sweatpants, but they're dirty, so I have on thick leggings with stocking feet.

"Got everything?" King calls.

I grab the pink sponge near my pillow and show it to him as I come out with the laundry bag. "Why do you want me to bring this?"

"Did your dad say anything?" he asks.

My stomach bunches up. I stretch it out, and my back unkinks one section at a time as my chest rises.

King looks away. He fixates on a squirrel halfway up a tree. The squirrel twitches its tail and freezes. King clicks his tongue at it, and the squirrel climbs down the tree— backward—and scampers through a bush.

I swipe King's arm. "You scared him off. You owe him an apology."

"Apology?" His jaw tenses. "You're the squirrel-talker. I only talk to rats. How 'bout I apologize to a rat and ask him to pass it on?" He breathes out hard and shakes his head.

"What's wrong?"

His eyes squint. "Nothing. I'm sorry."

It's not nothing, and we both know it. Today is special.

"Thanks for taking me."

Sabbath howls in the distance. *Shush*, I tell him. This is none of his business.

King shifts his feet. "Do you got the book? Time it's got returned. We made a deal."

The book.

I drop the laundry bag next to our near-empty rain catch and jump back in the tent. I lift my pillow to the mermaid and tell her it's time.

I zip up the tent when I come out, and King nods his approval at the book. The zipper snags at the top, a thread coming loose.

I blow soft on the thread and it wiggles alive. "You got a needle? I wanna fix it before it decides to unravel."

"Yeah, no thread though. Have to get some." King scratches three times on the tent again, but his scratches are rougher since this one's for Dad. "Mister. We'll be back in three or four hours."

I pluck at the thread. "That's not enough time for supplies. We should get some while we're out. Thread and water, and . . ." I run my tongue over my filmy teeth. "Toothpaste."

"Five hours," he tells my dad.

I stretch time through my hands. I need more.

King actually smiles. "We'll be back before dark."

Above his head, the youngest of the tree leaves jump in the wind. They're so easily entertained.

"Sit down," he says.

This is it.

He's gonna tell me we're not leaving tomorrow. He's changed his mind. This is our home, and it doesn't matter who's coming or what they take away. We're not gonna leave.

He must see some sort of spark in my eyes, cuz he clears his throat and smooths the front of his blazer. "I mean . . . I need to show you something before we go."

I sit on the ground while he picks out a short and sturdy stick. He sits beside me and draws a long oval in the dirt.

"What are you writing?"

"It's not a letter," he says. "It's a circle. For your berries."

He draws a line straight up that ends in a wall.

"This is the end of the Jungle."

"Why are you showing me?" I ask. "Are you going to leave me by myself?"

He pauses. His forehead wrinkles. "Course not. Watch." After the wall, the line turns and goes straight. He draws a rectangle and taps it. "Laundry." Then the line goes up again. He draws another rectangle. "Food." And another rectangle across from that. "Police." The line continues up to another rectangle. "Library."

He taps the library with the stick. "This is where you go if anything happens. Got it? For emergency."

I trace the lines with my eyes and nod.

He erases the lines with his foot and hands me the stick. "Draw it."

"I don't—"

His eyes go stern. "Draw it."

I take the stick and draw. Only I mix up some of the rectangles, and he has me draw it again. I get it right with a lucky guess.

I ask to draw it again. This time I dig the lines in my memory as I dig them in the earth.

He puts on his skullcap, black with a white cross, low over his eyebrows, then takes the laundry bag and throws it across his shoulder.

"Let's go."

Hamlet's drum music starts up again from down the hill—second morning call for breakfast. Too far to see. I hope the hamsters get some oatmeal.

"If we have time, can we see the hamsters?"

He tugs my hand and nods up the hill. "Let's go."

I step to leave, and that's when it becomes real to me.

I'm leaving.

I know we'll be back, but I can't help looking around to remember—my green tent and King's below us nestled by our tall soldier trees with trunks laced in ivy. Maybe it'd be easier to pretend this is a dream, and when I wake up,

I'll be home again.

"You sure we're not too early?"

"Nah," he says, "we'll get there when it opens. Won't be anyone."

I stop sleepwalking—almost drop the book. "But I need to see people. And the library. I need to see *everything*."

"Watch out for the log." He takes my arm and I step over it. "You will. It's just I got a kinda surprise, you know. Can't be no one there. Come on, now."

"For my birthday?"

His mouth lifts at one corner. "Don't go getting excited, it ain't much."

"But, still. A surprise. Will I get to see the Space Needle? Is it as sharp as one of your old needles, and does it really look like a spaceship? I can't remember."

"Don't know how sharp it is, but used to have dreams it was a spaceship that broke, and the aliens couldn't find a way home. Might see it, depending how far we get."

My head turns back to our tents. Already gone behind the thick green bushes and trees. Some leaves coloring in orange and red.

We stop at the blackberries. Leaves rustle low through the thicket, and my heart beats fast.

Don't seem like my bushes no more. Their canes arch above, twice the height of King, with toothed leaves and sharp spines that could tear into us both. A face pops into my head. Of a boy—nearly a man—with straight comb tracks in his blond hair.

King shakes one of my shoulders. "Just the squirrel. Remember? No one else."

I eat a large blackberry, and the image goes. I swallow it whole. "I know."

He tugs on his sleeves and slips through an opening I didn't know was there.

"The squirrel says it's okay?" I call out.

His hand appears through the bush, finds my arm. "Step in sideways and duck," he says. "Watch the thorns."

My legs don't wanna go, but I tell them to, and then before I know—he's somehow guiding me through, with two steps, three steps, four steps, five, and I'm on the other side without a scratch. Looks the same over here as it did over there. Nothing to be afraid of.

But I stay in back and follow his steps. He's so big no one will see me.

Trains rattle on their tracks and blow their whistles far below. A jumbo cargo plane flies high over us, so loud my body rattles. When it's gone, there's the hum of the *free*way. But all I see are trees, bushes, and grass. The sky surrounded by an umbrella of trees. For most of the life I remember. And I hope that's all I see until we get to the top.

But then I notice other things. Garbage. Plastic bags caught in trees, wadded tissues, dirty cardboard, empty soup cans, and a long white-yellow thing that looks like a balloon with no air—blown up over and over again until someone gave up. I know what it is. King pretends not to see it.

He's walking faster now. On guard. No one dares come to our side of the blackberries—they know it's King's. But this side is different. People come to do things they're not supposed to. I know what a gun sounds like, and I know when a scream isn't part of fun. I also know the difference between the ashy smoke from a warm fire and the sweet kind you hide from.

We pass a tree with another paper on it. King rips it off careful and shoves it in his pocket.

We climb now.

The hill is steep.

King's hand drops to the ground to help him climb better, and I do what he does. I try to keep up but have to kneel a minute. King comes back down to me.

"Forgot you're not used to exercise like this. We can rest. Not long, though. If you want your surprise."

I pant hard. "Tell me . . . what it is."

His eyes light up. "Not gonna spoil it now. What you thinking?"

I grab a branch above, pull myself to my feet. "Let's go."

He walks ahead. Up ahead. Toward the top of the hill, where a long concrete wall stretches forever. I've had dreams about that top, about climbing that wall. Nightmares, really. In my dream, I reach the top and look over to the other side. What I see is white, empty space. And I can't figure if it's a beginning or an end, and down below somewhere King yells for me to jump, so I do, but my feet never touch the ground.

"Come on!" he calls.

King goes over the wall every day. He leaves and comes back, so there must be another side. I keep my eyes up and chant each step.

To. The. Top.

To. The. Top.

To. The. Top.

King reaches the wall, and it's taller than he is. The squirrel is there, too. His tail flicks. A question.

Yes, I tell the squirrel. *I want to do this.*

King flings the laundry bag over the wall. The bag makes a soft thud.

Proof the ground exists.

He jumps with his arms stretched up, and his hands slap and hold to the top. He does a chin-up and surveys. Then he kicks his right leg up, and his foot lands on the top. He pulls himself up and squats, motions with his hand for me while he continues to keep watch.

I can't climb like that. But I walk the rest of the way and touch the slab. So cool on my hand.

The squirrel turns around in a circle.

"Aren't you gonna tell him he's done?" I ask.

King swings his legs to the other side, his firm stomach on the concrete, and reaches both arms down. "Who's done? Grab my hands."

I stand on my toes and reach up. A hand's-width gap

between us. "The squirrel. He was watching out for us. I can't reach your hands."

"Stop playing. C'mon, jump."

The squirrel is watching us now. "I'm not playing. If you're not gonna tell him, I will. Good job, squirrel." The squirrel flicks its tail again, then runs away.

King shakes his head. "Fine. Now, jump."

"I can't with my book."

"Throw it here. I'll catch."

I slip out the book and position it carefully between King's open hands. And. Toss.

He catches it and sets it beside him.

"Now jump."

I do, but miss his hand. I try again—our fingers connect. Shake. Can't hang on. I bend and steady my hands on my knees. Catch. Breath.

"Go at it again," he says.

"What's on the other side? Do you see anything? Any trees?"

King perches up on the concrete. "Sure, I see trees."

"Bushes? Grass?"

"Naturally."

"Anything else?"

"I see the Space Needle from here."

I snap up. "You're a liar."

"Come see for yourself. I see the Space Needle, the city, the shipyard and the bay—"

"The ocean?"

"From high up here you can see everything. Except our tents."

"Is that my surprise?"

"You get more than that. If you come up."

My back tingles. "Any people? Do you see any people?"

"Some cars—but with people who don't pay no mind. I told you it's early. We're clear." He gets onto his belly again and reaches down. "Come on."

Cars. I remember the soft fabric of the cushion on my cheek. Dad putting my blanket with the yellow stars on top of me. Hard walls protecting us from the wind and the wet as we slept. Then one day—an empty curb. Where our car used to be. We walked in the cold. Just the two of us. Legs tired. To find our car with my blanket. Then King, who led us here.

"You wanna see the Space Needle or not?"

I launch into the air, my legs weightless.

King grabs one of my hands with both of his, and for a moment I hang free.

"Climb!" he says.

I tuck in my knees and lean back, feet against the wall. King as my rope. King always my rope. But I'm older and heavier than I used to be. The soles of my boots grip the gritty concrete. I throw my loose arm up over my head and clasp onto his hands. One foot and another I climb. King's arms bulge between elbow and shoulder. My foot clears the top, and I straddle over to the other side. King steadies me.

His hands around my waist make me shiver, and I don't want him to let go. He doesn't notice. At least I don't think. He surveys around, then his shoulders relax and he loosens his grip from me. "What you think? Are you breathing?"

I am.

I have to force my eyes past his full-color lips, and the landscape sprawls in front of me—farther than I've ever seen.

Endless full pages.

Infinity.

King extends his arms at his sides like he's going to take off. The hoodie beneath his blazer matches the sky. "Feel like a bird, don't you?"

No. A ghost ascending to heaven. Seeing back through my life and peeking in at everyone else's. The morning light shines on the big cluster of glass buildings, and they glitter like the locket around my neck. Just like a fairyland.

I remember the city now, and all its tall buildings. They look small from this distance, but the Space Needle is easy to pick out. "What's that?" I point. "It's new."

"A Ferris wheel. You remember all this? You were a kid. Both of us."

"You were never a kid."

"Guess not."

"I'm not either."

"Naturally. Got your feel now? Wanna go back?"

I close my eyes and hear the familiar sounds—the trains, the planes, the trucks. That humming. I open. I see them all. And there's the *free*way. All those cars. Going. So fast. Going where so free?

"It's rush hour," he says.

"What's that?"

"Rushin' to get to work, you know. Lose their jobs if they don't." He spits over our side of the wall. Not a natural spit. One you have to force out of you. "Look at 'em all rush. Some gotta do it more than others. I had to get out *before* the rushing, so everyone could see my signs. Got 'em wanting a mattress even if they didn't need one."

"I doubt it was the sign they noticed."

He looks at me and smiles. "What do you—" He stops himself.

In a single movement, he drops down several feet to the other side.

He holds up his arms. "This. Is. Beacon Hill."

I take his lead and look around. Sure looks like a world I used to know—with streets, and cars, and shops, and everything. Still here after all this time. Not a ghost town. Every color represented. Not just blue, brown, and green. A different world. With real people. All that separated us was a wall.

I look from where we came, and I see garbage, though I know that's not what's beneath. Dad. With our tent that needs mending. My rock garden, which needs no water. And two buckets that need filling—one for cleaning, one for drinking. Out to the shipyard—there's so much water my scalp itches. I want to bathe my head in it.

Kings smiles. "Ready to see the world?"

I've been waiting.

5

"NATURALLY, YOU GOTTA KEEP your name to your-
self," he says. "If anyone asks you. No need to make yourself
familiar. Remember."

I keep my head down. Focus on the sidewalk and King,
enough for now. "Don't you think I know that? I'm a ghost,
right?"

He inspects his blazer. Brushes off the front. "I'm just
sayin'."

I smile at how good he looks in his blazer. "Why are you
dressed so nice?"

"Gotta be. I'm with you."

I concentrate on my surroundings. Allow my eyes to
drift past the sidewalk to the street—bare, not covered in

trees—exposed. I walk behind King and pull down my knit cap as low as his.

I can do this.

A car passes close enough to disturb the air around me. I move to the side, away from the flat-rocked street, and cross my arms in front of me. Forgot how fast cars move when they're right up beside you. When the next one comes, I'm ready. The car is small and bright yellow, and the driver's a woman who gives no mind to anything but what's straight ahead of her. If I had a car like that, I'd pay attention.

Shops line our side of the street. All kinds. For food. Cutting hair. Fixing cars. Coffee. Each one flashes familiar, but not quite real enough to remember. I'm pulled to what's on the other side: boxes of real solid houses with glass and brick and wood. The prettiest have gardens with real flowers. I don't know why you'd ever have a house without one, but some don't, and my eyes wander to those that do. I feel funny looking at them. The houses keep staring. Not at me, I don't think, but King is distinguishing in his blazer.

"What you looking at?" he asks.

"The windows over there. You think we can make more windows in our tent?"

"People build windows to look out. Forget about the looking-in part. No matter how they curtain up, someone can always figure a way to look in."

A loud beeping starts, and I jump.

"Watch out," he says, holding me back from a wide alley.

"A semi is backing up."

We cross the street to go around the truck, and I get smaller as we get close to the houses. I keep small until we cross the street again. The white bag sways across King's back.

"Don't you have laundry?" I ask.

"Only girls have as much laundry as this."

"I could do it myself once you show me."

He turns around—his mouth a straight line. "You won't need to. Once we find another place."

Someone comes up ahead. A man, maybe. Tall in a suit. Yes, a man. As he gets closer, I rotate around King, feeling like the second hand on Dad's watch, until King is between the stranger and me. The man's brown leather shoes are in a hurry and pass us quick. I don't look behind.

I reposition in back of King, who turns his head this way and that, then holds the bag with both hands. That means his knife is free in his pocket. He's not concerned, so I won't be.

Across the street, we pause at a ghost of a house with a big yellow machine roaring on top of its remains.

"Bulldozer," I say. As yellow as the stapled paper on the trees. I saw it in a book once, or maybe even for real one time. I can't remember. Memories get mixed up sometimes. I shiver as the bulldozer scrapes the ground, pushing splintered wood and chunks of cement into a pile. Louder than I ever imagined.

Once upon a time,
A house crumbled.

King wiggles my hand, and I realize mine is stiff. "It's not an end," he says. "Bet you anything the people who bought this place are gonna build something bigger."

"What about who lived there?"

"Found some other place. Making their own ending. How we make ours."

"What's gonna happen to the Jungle?"

He shrugs. "Put a fence around it probably. Not our business. Look. Over here." He points to a sign that reads *Coin Laundr.* The *y* missing. The place King cleans our clothes.

He opens the door. "See? It's open."

No one else is around. A line of machines down the narrow hall. None of them in use. All of them the same, except a rectangular one in the back, taller and brighter. I step.

"Rain, that's just shiny junk. I'll take you to a real place to eat."

Junk? My stomach growls again. I go to the machine and put my hand on the glass. Memories of junk machines come back. Chocolate bars, chips, and candy. Gum—the worst of all—something you put in your mouth, then spit out. Not food at all.

Oh. MoonPies.

"Can I have a MoonPie?" I ask.

"You've had it before?"

"Used to for breakfast sometimes. Please?"

"Chocolate or banana?"

"Banana."

King goes to the machine and inserts some coins, presses some buttons. The twirly wires push my pie forward. I squat near the swing door at the bottom and wait, place my book on the floor. I test out the door to make sure it's working. The plastic wrapper catches on the end of the wire, and I watch it swing like the bottom door's doing. King bangs the front of the machine, and it drops. I reach in and pull the wrapper open at the seams. Round and yellow as the moon. I break the MoonPie in half and hand him a piece.

King consumes it in two giant bites without tasting anything. A crumb lingers at the corner of his mouth, and I reach over to brush it, but he beats me to it.

He squints his eyes at me.

I take a small bite. Graham, marshmallow, waxy banana. I wait until the sweet marshmallow melts away on my tongue before I take another bite.

"Is this my surprise?" I ask.

"No."

I take another bite, a little larger, then wrap it back in the plastic. In my pocket to share with Dad later.

King picks up the bag of laundry before I can stop him. I wanted to do it. I open my mouth, but then close it. I'm far from being a child, and that's what I'd sound like if I argued. He might take me back home.

He opens the top of the machine and dumps it all in. He shakes, shakes, and drops the bag in, too, and closes the lid.

More coins from his pocket get the machine going. How many coins does he have?

"Aren't you supposed to put in soap? There's some boxes here in the machine. See? Bottom row. This purple one says it has lavender. Would be nice to smell like lavender."

"Nothing wrong with how we smell. Are you ready for your present?"

"I've been waiting."

King points to a door near the junk machine. "In there."

"You hid it there?"

"Go see. But first take off your boots."

I do as he says, and line them side by side. I open the door a crack. "It's all dark."

"You can't see nothing?"

"No."

"Well, shoot, I guess you don't have no present, then."

"You're lying. I know there's something."

"If you think so, go take a look."

I open the door wider and step into the cave. My heart beats so fast Mom's locket might bounce off my chest. Might even open. My eyes change to the dark, and I see something. A sink, a mirror, a toilet. But no tub. Instead, a clear glass box stands in the corner. "What's that?"

His brow crinkles. "A shower. That's your present."

"Thank you. I love it."

"You don't know what it is. You don't remember."

I'm thinking.

"You have your sponge like I told you?" he asks. "It's a bath—with rain."

He reaches around me and flips a switch. A light comes on and blinds me for a sec. He takes off his own shoes, then goes to the box and opens a door. He pulls a knobby handle at the wall, and water bursts in a thousand tiny drops over his hand. Had to be pent up to explode like that.

"Rain," I say.

"Just what I said."

"No. *Rain*."

He shakes the water from his hand and wipes his face damp. Water beads glisten on his neck. "I told you to keep your name to yourself. Shouldn't be sayin' it out loud like that."

"My mom used to say with a name like Rain I'd be all right. Can't be wet or cold if you *are* the rain. It's the sort of name to say out loud."

The sound of water echoes around.

He shakes his head.

A paper sign is taped to the outer glass of the shower. "*Out of Order.* Why does it say that?"

King clears his throat. "To stop people from using it. Signs aren't for us."

I squint at the sign. In my head, the words change until it reads for me: *Happy Birthday.*

"What if someone comes?"

"I'll be out here. Push the lock in like this. See? So no one gets in." He takes something from his pocket. Not his blade. A washcloth. And tosses it to me. "Not much, but you can use it to dry your hair and such."

I take off my stocking cap, and my mermaid hair falls around me.

King stares. A look I've never seen on him.

My face reflects from the big mirror above the sink, and I try to see what he sees. How old I look. And that's just the top half of me.

He presses his lips together.

"Is it true what the Winterfolk say?" I ask.

"What?" His voice is scratchy.

"Am I yours? I heard them say it."

He sniffs tough to make his lip snarl.

A million times I've seen it.

"You ain't nobody's." He wipes his cheek dry with his sleeve. "Don't forget to lock the door."

6

I STRETCH UP MY arms in the shower, and I'm thin as a grass blade. The water trails down to soothe my back, always tender from this pebble or that. My feet are the dirt, and they're thirsty. I open my mouth and drink. Water on the inside, water on the outside. Never tried that.

I stay in my tent when it rains, zipped up tight to keep it dry. Mud gets in fast, as fast as mold grows. Black mold in corners and creases. Needs alcohol to scrub it out, and then more drying. Best to never let it in at all.

I'm all wet. Not one piece at a time—how I usually wash—but my whole body at once as if swimming. Rain presses my eyelids closed and tells me don't open. Not ever. It wants to shush me to sleep.

I open anyway, and the water blurs my seeing. I wonder—
if I step on the holes in the middle of the floor, if I can stop
the water from going down the drain. Then the water will
fill up this box, and I can teach myself to swim.

Four knocks on the door. *Four.* I shake the water off my face.
King? No.

He would've knocked three.

The knob rattles.

I shut the rain.

"King?"

The door bangs. I don't move. Not a single bit. There's
some yelling, but I don't hear words.

I stay quiet, like those nights from somewhere over the
blackberries—POP-POP!

Disappear.

Breathe in, not out. Breathe in again. And again. Lungs
full of air with nowhere to go. But farther in.

And I wait.

For King outside to whisper, *Not to worry. All safe.*

His words don't come, and I got to breathe. The blood's
too hot in my face. I breathe out. Slow as I can—a small leak.
No one could hear anything but the drips from my hair, and
I can't help that.

Not a single noise outside that door, but I still wait. Some-
time, someone will come. Someone with a key. I can't go on
standing here naked.

I open the glass door.

I use King's square of a cloth to dab the drops away. Then underwear, tank, sweatshirt, and the leggings. I put my ear to the door and listen. Only the whirl of the washing machine.

"King?"

I hear breathing. My own.

"King?"

I turn the knob. The lock pops open. I open the door a sliver.

The washing machine's louder now, and there's no one I can see. Doesn't mean there's no one there. I sure know that.

I open wider.

My *Fairy Tales* book is on the ground in front of the junk machine where I left it. Our washing still going. Nothing else changed except King. Disappeared. Which means I'll wait. Because I know he'll be back.

I get my pink sponge from the shower. Squeeze out the water to nearly dry, and place it in my pocket with King's cloth and the half pie of moon.

Where are my boots? They were right outside the door. I walk the room searching. King wouldn't take my boots.

BEEP-BEEP-BEEP.

My head jerks around, and I drop to the floor.

The washing machine stops. That's all it was. My washing's done. But my heart still beats fast. It wants to go to that time I crossed the blackberries. Hands grabbed. Legs pinned.

I shake my head and go to the washer to occupy my mind.

Our clothes are clean, and it's time to dry. On the other side are machines that say *Dryer,* and there's a button that says *Start.* Well, that's easy. I could dry them myself if I had King's coins.

I walk to the glass front of the laundry place in my stocking feet, and wait.

King wouldn't take my boots.

A gray woman in brown walks by, and I shrivel to the side—brown coat, brown skirt, brown shoes. Brown shoes that shine. Someone else walks by—orange penny shoes— not sure if a man or woman. Black heels click-click. Their stems wither away. There are black boots, but not mine. They have buckles. Mine have laces. None of those shoes are mine.

King wouldn't bang on the bathroom door, and he wouldn't take my shoes.

The library, he said. *This is where you go if anything happens.*

My skin crawls. This is something happening.

I twist up my hair to put on my cap, but my hair's still wet, so I put the cap in my pouch where it can keep dry. I pick up the book that's meant to return since I promised and snap it into my waistband beneath my sweatshirt. I step outside where it's bright. The door jingles as I leave. I flinch. Did it jingle when we came in? Why is it so loud?

A car screeches past, and I close my eyes.

My head buzzes, and I make myself breathe.

Alone. I've been alone before. Not outside the Jungle, but

I've been alone plenty. I know how to be alone.

The cement is cold through my stockings. Good. Will help me walk fast, cuz the faster I walk, the faster I'll get to the library and see King. Because nothing can happen to King.

I look far, but don't see him.

In front of me must be the street from King's map. The one that ends at the library.

"Those were *your* boots?"

I turn to a girl who leans against the wall. Her hair is black, tips dipped in purple. Her eyes nearly match those tips, but lighter. Violet. She's in a white dress. An actual dress. And the whitest white I've ever seen. The top part like a man's shirt with short sleeves, a wide black tie at the neck.

My sweatshirt is a man's—we're the same that way. But hers is a man's made for a woman. The bottom part stops just before her knees, where the laces of tall, black boots criss-cross down to her feet. Not my boots. Not mine anything. Her body fills her dress like mine would never fill my sweat-shirt. She must eat plenty. Not too much. The right amount.

"You saw?" I ask.

She pushes herself from the building. "Who wouldn't?" She points to my bootless feet. "They were yours, right?"

She bosses as a man does, but her lips are red. Lipstick. A large, black bag hangs from her shoulder. I bet she has lots of makeup in there. I wonder how old she is. Sixteen? Seventeen? She narrows her eyes. Questioning, maybe, about me.

Across the street, a sign with a hand flashes as red as her lipstick.

I ignore its warning and nod.

Someone took my boots.

"I'm so done with him," she says.

King? She doesn't know him. Or else she'd never say that.

"You'll get your boots," she says. "Your friend's more pissed than I am. The only reason I'm waiting is to give him what he had the nerve to put in my bag. That, and I never want to see his face again. I'm not doing it anymore."

King? The flashing hand across the street stops.

She takes in my wet hair and no-makeup face. "How do you know Cook?"

Cook.

The name hits my gut, and my blood drains. That must be what the gutters are for between the street and the sidewalk. There are no gutters between my trees.

"You do know him," she says. It isn't a question. Her face falls. "What did he do?"

Blond comb tracks. Too straight and too deep.

King said he was gone for good.

"You don't need to tell me," she says. Then she screams, but it's a quiet scream. Like some of the rocks back at home. "He's an asshole. And I'm an asshole for believing him. He saw your friend in there and told me to stay. Like a dog. Then he ran out with your boots, and your friend chasing."

The tips of her hair are the color of those berries.

I shake my head. It can't be him.

She leans back against the building. "Is that guy your boy-friend?"

I'm nobody's. He's nobody's.

"He seems nice," she says. "Nice enough to go after your boots. But you never know. Obviously." She looks my face over.

I try to look older. Stand straighter. Cock a knee like hers.

"I met him at a club. I thought he was nice. Special, even."

Special?

"I thought I could help him," she says. "He lives . . ."

I uncock my knee.

She looks me over, and an eyebrow raises. "Do you live around here?"

I nod.

"Where? I live in Queen Anne. I'm Matisse. What's your name?"

She talks too much. Trusts too much. How could she think he was nice? The soil beneath my trees would refuse to bury him.

She can believe.

Because her name is Matisse. She can say her name out loud. And she's from Queen Anne. The daughter of a queen. Bad things happen to princesses all the time, but they never expect it.

"Evil isn't special," I warn. "Don't wait for him."

I need to find King. I look up and down the street.

I take a step.

She holds my arm. "I believe you. And I'm sorry for whatever he did."

"It's not nice to talk about the past."

She leans her head to the side, and her purple tips brush her shoulder. "You can't walk in stockings. You'll hurt your feet."

Is it odd to walk in stockings? Maybe it's odd. Must be.

"Let me give you a ride. You could stay in the car while I wait for him. It's around the corner." She adjusts her bag. "I wish I could leave, but I don't have a choice. If I don't give this back, he'll never leave me alone. Afterward, I'll drop you off. Where do you need to go?"

I shake my head.

"You want to go after your friend, don't you?" she asks. "You're worried about him."

I fold my arms over my book.

"If it makes you feel any better," she says, "it looked like Cook was playing. I'm sure they'll be back soon."

My fist clenches around his name. "They're not playing. You should go."

She pulls at the tips of her hair. "I *wish*."

My hand jerks forward and covers her mouth. "It's not kind to wish."

Her eyes grow wide, and she steps away from me.

I clasp my hands behind my back. Focus on my toes. Rub my big one hard against the cement. I didn't mean to make her afraid.

"It's okay," she says.

And I look up at her.

"I'll go," she says. "After I give this to him."

"He wants it that bad?" I ask.

"Bad enough."

My words speak on their own. "Then give it to me."

She holds up her hand. "You don't even know what it is."

"Something he wants."

She clutches her bag, and her eyes think they know me. They say, *You're one of them.* As if I could ever be like him.

A car whirs past—as fast as my heart. To have something Cook wants. To take it.

I shake my head. "It could help my friend."

Her grip loosens. She looks around, then reaches into her bag. Looks around again and stuffs something in my front pocket.

She backs up quick. "You really don't care what it is, do you?"

"No."

I wait for her to leave so she doesn't see where I'm going. But she still looks at me.

Look away. I will her to.

I'd look away if someone was looking at me. But she's not. I cock my knee again. Hard.

She sticks her hand in her bag. Something else of Cook's?

"Why am I already regretting this?" she says.

I hold my pouch closed. I won't let her take it.

She pulls out a marker. Grabs my arm and pulls up my sleeve. I'm as surprised as she is.

"Do you mind Sharpie?" she says. She writes. On my arm. It tickles.

"That's your name," I say. "Matisse." I look up at her, and she seems more real now that her name is written. "How do you do that?"

She pauses. "Jesus." Then writes more furious. "This is my phone number. If anything goes wrong. I work at Spazz."

I'm sure my face is blank.

"Spazz Coffee?" she says. "On Second Ave."

"Do you want my name?" I ask. "On your arm?"

She offers the marker, but I push it toward her.

"Rain. R. A. I. N."

She pulls up her white sleeve.

I step close so I can watch her write the letters. One after the other. Until my name appears.

"That's me," I say.

I want to touch the letters on her arm. She's going to be looking at them later and be thinking about me. I feel as permanent as the marker—as solid as the concrete that runs down the street, as great as the wall we climbed, and as old as the hill that is our home.

"Do you have a number?" she asks.

"No."

"What about the number of a friend?"

I shake my head.

She presses the cap of the marker between her fingers, then slowly starts to put it back on. Like she's hoping for more.

"Wait," I tell her. "Will you write something else?" I look around for something to write on. Something people will see. I point to the cement under our feet. "There."

"What?"

I pull down my sleeve. "WINTERFOLK."

She nods and squats with her knees together to one side. She starts to write in big letters. She gets to the T, and I trace it with my toes. Two logs. That's all they are. One balancing on top of the other. If you took the bottom away, the top would fall down.

She frowns and finishes writing. "Is that how you want it?"

"Looks real, doesn't it?"

She stands and puts the lid on the marker. "Sure." She shakes her head. "Seriously. You have my number, right? Call me." She puts away her Sharpie. Waits for me to leave.

But I don't. I wait for her.

She shakes her head again and walks down the street. She's getting smaller. The word must be getting smaller, too.

"Can you still see it?" I yell.

"Call me!" she says back.

I keep watching until she turns the corner and I don't see her no more. I press my arm against my book and read again.

WINTERFOLK

I study the letters like a map that could take me back home.

I shiver.

The sign across the road turns red again, and I cross.

I gasp as gravel digs into my soles, but it doesn't stay. Just like people.

They come and they go. And the hurt goes away. Mostly.

I turn to look back at her, but she's really gone.

Was she ever here?

I lift my sleeve, and her name is across my flesh, as mine is across hers.

We are here.

I put my hand in my pocket and feel the thin plastic of a baggie. I pinch it as I step careful for ants and any other little thing. I don't want to feel them squish. As my innards now do when my fingers sink into something finer than salt or sugar. I pull the corner of the baggie out from my pocket, and it's as white as Matisse's dress.

What did I do?

I trip over the curb, and my head buzzes. What will *he* do when he finds out?

I shake my head to clear it.

Follow King's map.

Find King.

Get my boots back.

Think of the map.

Dig your feet into the map.

Ahead is a store on the same side as I am with posters of hot dogs and chili. Good. Just like King said.

I'm going the right way. Doing something right. Keep going.

I stare at the *Hank's Hot Dogs & Chili* sign. My stomach's squeezed tight, but even if I had King's coins and nothing else in my pocket, I couldn't eat anything of Hank's. I need to find King. Someone in Hank's alley pokes in a trash can. Has a souped-up cart on six decent wheels. Good luck.

Keep going.

Across is the police station. I walk on the balls of my feet and try not to look at that rectangle building. King says they have red-and-blue policing power, red for some and blue for others.

They stick it to you, he says. *That red-and-blue power. Stay away.*

I keep my head forward.

Ahead is like a museum with brown brick and lots of windows, but the sign over the door says *Beacon Hill Library*. I thump the book under my sweatshirt. I saw a picture of a library once with smiling people. Every single one of them. I smile like I'm supposed to. There's another sign posted on the door. *Shirts and shoes required.* I open the door since signs aren't for me.

A girl about King's age is at the front desk. Not noticing me, of course. She doesn't wear glasses like the library ladies I saw in picture books when I was little. Not at all like in the pictures. Her brown skin is darker than her hair—cut short like a boy—and her shape is like most boys, too.

She talks to a little kid who does have glasses, as well as droopy jeans she keeps in place with her hands in her pockets.

"I'm sorry, but you can't check out any more books until you pay your late fee," the library lady says. "After that, you can check out five books and try to return them on time."

I glide past them—my feet too quick to notice—surprising how fast without shoes. And then I see the books. All those books. King never told me how many. He's been stingy. Row after row. Don't seem to stop. I reach out my hand and run my fingertips across them—all different colors and sizes. How many pages, how many words? How many stories?

King said to look for the nature section. That's where he'd be. I scan the cards on the stacks. *Research, History, Science, Mathematics, Computers, Philosophy, Poetry, Fiction, Fantasy, Horror, Nonfiction, Children's, Nature.* In the back corner with the posters of tree frogs and leaves.

King isn't there.

I squeeze my book and read the card again to be sure. *Nature.*

The librarian gets up from her chair. I sit against the wall on top of my feet. Can't let her see my feet, or she'll know I don't belong.

He'll be here. I know he will. I close my eyes, ignore the bulge in my front pocket, and reach to the books. Some titles bubble beneath my fingers, others lie flat and unseen. My hand rests on one of the unseen ones, and I pull the binding free from the shelf, set it on my lap, and rub its glossy cover.

Eyes open. See the ocean.

I open to pictures of tropical fish. I squeeze my hair and a water drop falls to the green carpet. My book of fairy tales digs in my ribs, but I can't take it out yet. I lean my head back against the wall and want to sleep beneath this roof held up by words. My feet and all my fat pig toes snuggle and rest. What's the story about pigs? The first fairy tale King ever brought me. The smart one built his house with bricks, but bricks can be bulldozed. He should've built it with words instead.

"Rain."

He's breathless. My boots hang from his right hand. His hair is in blue-black waves—a storming ocean.

"Your eye's swelling," I say.

"Your hair's wet."

Because it's been crying, I want to say, but I don't say that. I'm where he told me to be. And he has my boots. He got them without me having to do anything. If King found out what I did—

"Why'd you take my boots?" I ask.

I know he didn't take them, but I don't know if he'll tell the real truth.

"I didn't. I was gettin' them back."

"From?" I ask.

"Someone I used to know. Thought it funny."

I itch my arm. The one with the name. "Who?"

Tell me.

King shifts his weight.

My stomach flutters. Don't know if it's me or what he might say that does it.

His face tenses. He stretches his fingers wide across my shoes, and the tension ripples from his face to his hands. He sits down next to me and sets my boots in front. "Cook."

The fish book falls to my lap.

"You said the fucker was gone."

His face blanches. "Don't talk like that. I thought he was. I really did. But you don't gotta worry. He was just pranking."

"Why? Cuz he's a funny guy?"

His jaw clenches. "No. I don't know why I said that. He won't be back this time."

"You use your blade again?"

"He won't be back." His eyes float down to the book. "What you reading?"

I point to the fish. My finger shakes at what he might have done, or what he might not have done. I don't know what I want more.

"Amphiprion percula," he says.

I concentrate on the fish. "Clownfish. Funny fish."

"What about this one?" He holds my finger steady and points to another one. *"Centropyge aurantonotus."*

"Flaming angelfish. You got me this book once. Don't you remember? Had it for a long time."

"I remember," he says.

I slip my finger from him. "It's a children's book."

He folds his hands together. "I know."

"I had this book *too* much time. Didn't know there were so many books." I smell the fish book to check for home, but nothing distinguishes it.

He looks around. "Too many books. You bring it?"

"What?" My cheeks flame. Not like the glow of an angel, or that angelfish swimming on the page—blue with a golden stripe on top.

I clutch my pouch, and sweat beads above my upper lip.

His forehead wrinkles. "The book."

"Oh." I wipe the sweat from my lip.

He doesn't know.

He picks up one of my empty boots and taps my foot with it. "Steady," he says.

The books tower around me. They hum. *Once upon a time. Once upon a time.* They want to tell me their stories.

He looks to my stomach. "Your book in there?"

I hug my knees. "Yes."

I pull at my wet hair.

"You promised you'd give it," he says.

"You promised he was gone."

His eyes go hard. "Put on your boots. We're going back to camp."

"I don't want them."

He points to his swelling eye. "I got 'em back for you."

I press my chest to my thighs. "I didn't ask you to."

"Okay," he says. "How many books you want? Can't take too many. Be quick."

This can't be how today ends.

"I want them all," I say.

He laughs. Fake.

"Borrow them," I say. "Like anyone else."

"You need a library card," he says, "and an address with proof to back it. You ain't got proof of nothing."

"We can draw the map like you showed me."

"Put on your boots."

"Why don't you show them?" I say.

"It's got to be an address with numbers, like, or names so they know where to collect the fines if you don't bring them back. You'd get way fined up if they knew about you."

"I'll promise them."

He pushes his hair back, but it drops forward again. "Get your stuff on."

I put on the boots. Then I do as King says and twist my wet hair up into my knitted cap.

"The book?" he says.

"Not a chance."

"Then I'm not getting more."

"Whatever." I stand. "Let's go."

King walks on the near side of the librarian. She smiles at him. I grab King's hand, and he clenches it hard.

I bet she can write.

My feet slip and slide in my boots as we walk down the hill, and my stomach groans. I don't know if Cook is doing this to my stomach, or if it's because I'm mad at myself or King, or if Hank's sign ahead is getting the better of me.

My stomach complains again, and King looks sidelong at me.

He lets go of my hand and takes a deep breath. "You hungry?"

"I don't know." I prefer to be hungry over afraid, and I don't want to be mad at King. I make up my mind to be hungry. "My dad said not to ask for anything."

He laughs. "That didn't stop you from the MoonPie or the books. Anyway, you're not asking. I am. Are you hungry or not?"

"Maybe for the chili."

"Yeah, me too. Wait here."

I stay on the sidewalk with my back to the police station while King walks into Hank's. A siren sounds behind and locks my knees. I clench my front pocket, but my book breathes next to my skin, so I do, too. That siren's not for me. That library lady couldn't see my book, not with King there. No one can see nothing. And I doubt King's sticking up Hank.

Car wheels spin behind me on the street, along with their lights and sirens, and then they're gone and I'm still breathing.

King comes out with a yellow paper bag, not looking at the station. He swings his arms like he never heard the siren and pulls out a container. It warms my hands.

"Careful, it's hot," he says. "Listen. Don't worry about him. I'm sorry I got mad. I'm just hungry."

I find myself repeating my dad. "Hungry's not an excuse."

"I know," he says.

"And you've got to stop telling me what to do. I'm too old for that."

He kicks a small stone. "I know how old you are. Believe me."

"Then tell me. Why are you sure he won't be back?"

"Cuz he won't, and I don't wanna talk about it when I'm about to eat."

Water runs down the gutter beside the street, and I shudder.

His eyes shift to the bag. "This used to be a fish 'n' chips place. Remember eating some of that? Used to get it for you sometimes. Same owner, Hank. Known him a long time. Told him he should add salmon to the menu, but he never did. Now it's hot dogs 'n' chili."

I open the lid to the chili, and the steam burns my face. My stomach responds to the smell of the chili.

Yes, I was only hungry.

"Hank—he knows you? Did he ask about your eye?"

King shrugs.

"I like fish 'n' chips," I say, "but the chili smells good."

"The fish 'n' chips was better."

I tilt the cup to my lips. It nearly burns, but the tomato meat is surprisingly delicious.

King reaches in the bag and pulls out a dog. "The fish 'n' chips cost more, though. These are four for a dollar. A bargain." Half of it goes in his mouth. I know he's not tasting.

I sip slow this time, and my mouth fills with cocoa and cinnamon from the chili.

Up ahead at the corner is the same man with the souped-up cart. He has a brown sign, cardboard, but I can't see what it says. Guess no one else can either, cuz the cars keep passing.

I swallow. The full bite goes down to keep my stomach quiet. "When you worked those mattress signs—you said people took notice?"

King takes another bite, and the dog is gone. "Naturally."

My elbow points to the man. "Maybe he should dance. So people can see him. We could tell him to dance."

King stops chewing, and I know I've said something wrong. "He shouldn't have to," he says, and then he's off.

I hurry to press the lid on my chili and catch up to King while my feet slide in my shoes again. We get close to the man—trim beard, drippy eyes. I read his sign. We pass.

His sign.

And King gives him something—his bag with three dogs

left. This time I see the sign.

HOME.

Not *homeless*. *HOME*. Like it vanished, and he's asking where it went. Makes me think of that bulldozer with splintered wood and broken stone.

Once upon a time there was a home.

And there were swing sets and water fountains and sandy beaches. Four walls with a roof, and a fence.

I want to smack his sign. IT'S GONE! He should forget.

He leans over his cart for privacy and eats one of the dogs. I know how hungry he is by how slow he eats.

And I imagine the Winterfolk here. Lined side by side on the road for as long as you can see. All holding that sign. *HOME*. Cars drive by with no notice, except for one who yells at them to dance.

How do you make someone see you?

"We can't go home yet," I tell King.

He tucks his empty hands in his blazer. He looks at that sign, too. Then he narrows his eyes the way he does to blank out everything.

Including me.

My fingers tingle around my cup, going from warm to hot to hotter from the chili, but I keep them there as they go numb.

King's eyes clear, and he looks up and down the street. For Cook? Police?

I squeeze the cup.

Air huffs from his lips, and his eyes fill up with me.

I adjust the cup in one of my hands for a cooler spot above the chili, and my fingers tingle alive again.

"Okay." He sees my smile and smiles back at me. "We can leave the laundry. No one'll take it. We still have time. Know if your dad is going to the market today?"

"No, he's going to make more bracelets. Said he might teach me when I get back."

"Don't you know how already?"

My chili-warmed fingertips glide against the necklace at my neck. Of course I know. I've been watching for years.

"Yes, but he wants to teach me and I'm going to let him. Are we going to the market?"

He shrugs. "Maybe. Eat your chili. All of it."

"All?"

My stomach will complain tonight as it shrinks back up, and I hate to muffle the sound under my blanket. Dad will blame *me*. As if I can help it.

"Yeah. All. Cuz we're gonna walk far and fast. But you've gotta stay with me. You won't find your way back by yourself."

"Let me first take off these boots," I say. "It's the only way I'll keep up with you."

7

MY FEET LOOK BIGGER out here than when they're buried in soil, and I like how they bend when I walk—first my heel against the hard pavement, and then the cushion under my toes, missing the tender middle altogether. My boots bounce across my shoulder. One in front, one in back, tied together by their laces.

King points to the next store coming up on my side. "Look what's in there."

I run to the window, and guess what I see? Baby cats, three of them, curled up sleeping in a wood box—one black, one white, and one orange.

"I like the orange one," I say. "With the scrunched face. Look how long her fur is. Must take forever for her mom to clean and comb. I bet she doesn't fuss. Is her mom in there?"

"Don't know."

"Do you think we can go in? I've never pet a cat."

King opens the door, and a bell rings—*ding-a-ling*. "Don't say anything to get you noticed."

The store smells like Hamlet's bucket of hamsters.

A man looking like a stuffed koala with big ears stands behind a table in back. He looks up at King, but I do a good job with him not seeing me.

Rows of bags, boxes, and little cans sit beneath a sign that says *Pet Food*. I know it means *food for a pet*, and not to pet the food like I wanna do—pet each bag, box, and can that will keep the kittens alive. I don't look at the price tags.

"How much does a cat eat?"

"A bag a day," King says.

I look sharp at him. "If I ate cat food, that bag would last me a month."

"Good to know," he says.

I bump his arm, and a corner of his mouth curves up. He tilts his head, and his hair covers the rest of his smile.

Over us is a *Toys* sign. Feathers, long stringy things, scratchy boards, and balls line the shelves on either side of us. Must like to play. I could make some of those things if I had a cat.

We pass a couple of empty cat boxes, then one with a full-grown orange cat that backs into a corner. Hair sticks up and big eyes reflect. Cats are known to see the otherworldly.

"Not to worry. I'm not going to hurt you," I say.

And then I lean over the box with the sleeping kitties and find the orange one.

"Will they let me pick her up?"

"How do you know it's a girl?" King says.

"She's the smallest. See?"

He blinks. "That's not always the case."

As far as I know, it is. "Can I pick her up?"

He looks behind at the man, who must be harmless, because King nods.

I reach in and scoop up the kitty as gentle as I can and hold her in the space between my neck and shoulder.

King takes the boots off my shoulder, and my shoulder rises.

I bury my fingers in her deep fur.

"She's so soft. Is she still asleep?"

King nods.

"Of course she is. I'd be, too." I lean my cheek against her. "Her breath smells sweet. You sleep all day cuz you're in here? Ever sneak out at night and play with those feathers? I bet you do. No one sees you, do they? You should see my rock garden. I collected them all myself. You'd like them. Wanna come with me? If you polish them, they'll tell you a secret."

"No."

I hardly heard, but I know what King said, and his eyes keep looking out the window with not much on his face to tell me anything. I've tested him. But I'm not done.

"I can share my food with her, if that's your worry. And it's not like a barking dog—or even a hamster. Plus, she'd keep me company. You know I don't like being alone."

He stuffs his hands in his blazer pockets. "You're not alone."

I nuzzle the cat. "You know what I mean."

King says no more, and I say no more about what it's like when he's gone. How the leaves of the trees rustle in whispers, and I answer them back.

I give the kitten a light squeeze before I lay her down how she was, still sleeping, and not ever knowing I was there.

But then the cat's eyes open. Green. She looks at me.

Meow.

King's arm dangles down with my boots, and the laces swing on their own with no one telling them.

I turn my face from King so only the cat sees me, and I tell her I'll be back. She doesn't got to worry. I'll find some way to get money, and when no one's looking I'll come. I remember how to get here. If anyone else comes, she's to be disagreeable. Her claws will protect. They're nearly as long as mine.

She nods her head. She understands I'm not really leaving. That I'll do almost anything. And then she closes her eyes again.

I put the boots across my shoulder—boots heavier than a

baby cat. My shoulder lowers, but I breathe in and ask.

"Where next?"

"My eye still swollen?"

"Yeah, and purple now." His whole face would turn purple if he knew what was in my pocket.

He adjusts the cap over his eyebrows so the cross is straight and slows his walk. "You ever go out at night? Like you thought that cat might?"

I stumble, and King notices. "Out? What would I do out?"

"Don't know," he says. "Collect rocks? Take care of the stars."

My laugh turns to a croak. "You'd know if I went out."

"Naturally. Still." He touches a finger to his puffy eye.

"You should put a cold rag on that."

"I know. When we get back, but I'm serious. Don't go out at night, 'kay?"

"Why? You said he's gone."

He touches another part of his eye and winces. "Yeah, but he has friends—not all that smart."

"Can't be as smart as you."

"Course not. Does all kinds of things to get noticed. *Wants* to be noticed. See that bench up there? Would do a somersault right over it just to turn heads."

"Can you?"

He smiles. "Who you think showed them?"

"Show me?"

He clicks his tongue. "Just told you it's not smart. Gives a rush like racing down Suicide Hill, but not smart."

Suicide Hill's where he watched horse races in the good years when he was little. They'd race horses down a steep hill and across a river. Some stumbled, some fell, some died.

"But you're not like that." I stop and look around. "Come on, no one's here."

"No one you can see." But he bends his knee and pulls a leg back into a stretch.

"Come on. I've never seen a flying somersault before, and I know you're not a showoff."

King stretches his arms across his front now.

"Can you do a somersault with a blade?" I ask. "I can hold it."

His eyes catch me. Knows I want to see what's on his blade. "It's folded. Won't stick me."

He secures his skullcap and blows into his palms. Then his eyes go hard and narrow on that bench. He pounces forward faster than I've ever seen. Can barely see his feet. Running so fast he'll never come back.

I crush into my book. If he keeps going, I'll run after him.

Before he slams his shins on the bench, he leaps into the air and spins like a rising star never to come down again. But he does. That star falls on the other side to a graceful landing. I can't help myself. I run over and hop onto the bench to stand over him.

"Why your eyes so big?" he says. His energy shining. "You didn't think I could do it?"

"I know you can do anything."

He laughs and stands up straight. Straightens his jacket.

Then everything changes at once.

He grabs my wrist, pulls me down hard off the bench. I ready up to scratch, but stop. He must have a reason. His eyes are in slits, and I follow their path across the street.

Blond comb tracks.

The ground swallows my feet as it does in my nightmares. But this is real. King tugs on my arm. He doesn't know how my feet can't move, and how I can't say anything—how the words catch the way they do when I try to write anything.

Somehow we run.

King grabs my boots, and we turn a corner and run down a hill. Only my toes touch the ground. Almost flying. He drops my hand, and we use our arms to pick up speed. Look both ways across the street and we cross over. Down another. Behind me, I try to see, but don't see nothing. Hard to catch breath. But King's still running, so I do. There's a bus at the corner—starts to leave, but King waves.

The door opens and King helps me in. Pulls out more coins.

The bus starts up, and I fall down on black rubber. On all fours I can't move. Not with the bus moving under me and someone chasing.

King holds out his hand.

The bus is too unsteady for me to reach out to him.

"Will you hold on a minute, please?" asks King.

I think he's talking to me.

"Wait till she gets her seat?"

He's talking to the driver.

The bus stops. I scramble up and King finds a seat. Him next to the window. Looking out. Surveying.

My hands shake on my shaky knees. From the bus, I think. Or from running.

I put my head on his shoulder. "Where we going?"

"Uptown."

Bus is half full. So many people so close. I shiver.

"That wasn't him," I say.

"It was. I need to get more money. Wasn't planning on the bus."

I lift my head to look at him. "Was one of his friends."

He turns his face to the window with the light shining. My boots are on his lap with his hands on top, fingers stretched wide.

"It wasn't him," I say. "He didn't look hurt." Though all I saw were the comb tracks.

King slams his fist against the side of the bus. I don't care.

"Does he want my boots?" I ask. "He can have my boots."

"Your boots?"

My front pocket crinkles, and my stomach gurgles sick.

I sit back against the seat and close my eyes. Try not to feel the bus move beneath me. I taste a bit of sour tomato from the chili. I concentrate on the book that rests on my stomach.

The bus goes up and down. And that tomato does not like me.

King knocks three times on the hard cover of my stomach. Too close to my pouch.

I open my eyes. I should tell him what I did. But if I do, King will go after him. I know he will.

"It's me he wants," he says. "I jacked him up."

My guilt weighs in with the tomato. "Where are we going?"

The bus turns, screeches, and I cover my mouth.

"Remember that first night you both slept in my tent?" he asks.

He's trying to distract me like he always does when I feel sick.

"Your dad—*one* night, he said. Kept his arms around you. Talked to himself. But I'm glad. I'm glad it was two nights, then three. *Time goes fast*, he said, *can't keep track of time no more.* I think he's right. Time's gone fast." He leans his head against the window. "You know I have a sister? Near old as you, now, I guess. She liked to sing."

I sit forward. He's never talked about a sister.

King looks out the window and squints his eyes in the sun. "People sure noticed her."

The bus jerks to a stop, and I put my hand to my mouth.

A man and woman pass us by and get off. The doors sound

a gush of air as they close back up.

This time it's my turn to distract him. I swallow the bile.

"I'm sorry I made you do the flying somersault. To get you noticed."

He shrugs me off. "You know I don't do nothing I don't want. Just a few more stops for us."

I look out. The squatty buildings are bigger now, so much bigger than the trees I know. I've read about rain forests—the trees so big you can't see their tops. I can't see the tops of these buildings, not from the bus at least. In the pictures I saw, there'd always been light shining through the leaves. These buildings have more windows than I've ever seen, but there isn't any sort of light coming down on me.

"Is this where people work?" I ask.

"Work and live. Live and work."

Each window looks the same to me. "Looks like a lot of jobs. You think there's one for blowing glass?"

King stares out the window. The sun sparkles yellow through it.

"We had the prettiest Christmas ornaments. Said Mom was the heart and he was the breath. I always liked that. He doesn't feel right without her."

"Naturally," he says.

"He used to make glass beads, too. Now they're from the store. Says he can't be the breath without the heart, but if he . . . I don't know. I'm not wishing. I wouldn't do that."

His eyes lock on mine. "You should wish."

"Don't say that."

The bus stops hard at a red light and pushes me forward against the seat.

People of all kinds rush across the street, walk fast or run—girls painted pretty as tropical birds—all with somewhere to go. No one telling them where to go or what to do. The bus starts up again, along with my stomach.

I pick at the bottom of Dad's sweatshirt where there's a small tear. "Did he ask for wine? Don't get it." I stick a fingernail through the tear. "We need thread, though, before the tent falls apart. It will soon. We can't forget the thread. And water."

"We'll get lots." He nudges my elbow. "Here we are. Our stop is coming."

I ready my legs and hold my book to me. I start to get up when the bus stops, and hang on to the seat to keep myself from falling. King taps my back to get me going, and I run down the path to the door before it opens. Then I'm out on solid ground again. King behind me.

Up around—not a rain forest at all. The buildings on either side reach up. They try to cut orderly lines in the sky, but those buildings do have tops. I see them. And they can't reach far enough to cut.

"Will we have time to walk back? I don't want to take the bus. I don't like how it moves under me."

"We'll see."

"Where we going?"

"Need to make a stop up here a couple blocks."

"What we stopping for?" I ask.

"Money."

"Good. I need money."

"What you need money for? I already said I'd get supplies. Plus, this ain't that kind of store. You can't go in."

"What kind of store is it?"

"Up here." He points to a store with blackened windows. Has a sign above with a pair of sheer stocking legs spread out in an upside-down V. Between them is a big blue sign with a right-side-up V. The red-ribboned ankles balance on top of the V like they're doing the splits—feet pointed gracefully like a lady to the tips of netted toes.

My toes strangle in my stockinged leggings. "King?"

He sets my boots on the ground. "You stay out here and don't say anything. I mean it."

I crouch against the building next to my boots while he walks through an arched entry that leads to the front door. I pull at the tips of my stockings to give my toes more air, then lean my head around the corner to the entry.

"King. What brings you here?" a bald man says at a ticket window. He reminds me of a ferret how he moves his head here and there.

"Hey, Bob. Is Denise around? I need to ask a favor."

He bobs his head. "I heard you traded in your needles. Is that true?"

"Naturally. She back there?"

"Because I don't want any needles in my house. Remember?" He bobs his head again and fixes his eyes.

"I know. She here?"

"She's here."

King reaches to open the door.

"Hey, King," the man says.

"Yeah?"

"Good seeing you."

King nods and opens. I lean farther—just in time to see through the open door—a big blue V onstage with a pole stuck in the middle. The door closes, but not all the way. A finger's worth would pry it back open again. Bob's head turns toward me, but I escape and tuck my chin down in my neck.

I pull my sweatshirt over my knees to create a tent for my legs, tucking the bottom under my feet, and everything held tight in my pocket. I breathe hot air down in the tent. Warm over my caving chest.

What's King doing?

A movement from the corner of my eye catches my attention. A mound of blanket on the pavement not too far from me against the building. Another movement beneath. Has no cardboard sign. Must be trying to sleep. Don't know how anyone can with all these legs walking by to do their business. When I was small, all I saw of people were their legs. Had to look far up to see their faces. Mom wore long, red skirts that wrapped around her legs.

Her face gets farther and farther from me.

I peek around the corner again. Head Bob is gone, and that door's still ajar.

My hands and knees move forward, and I let them take me. I grip the part of the door that sticks out and wedge in my fingers until it gives without a sound. I pull it open until the stage appears again with the pole and the V. The lights above the stage are red, and drum music plays in deep, slow beats.

I know what live drums sound like, and these ones are fake—like King's radio that plays music from somewhere far away.

A woman walks onto the stage, and I almost lose the door. I hold on tight again. Brown hair and silky robe. One hand on her hip; the other at her mouth with a cigarette. She's not dancing.

The drum beats louder and she turns around slow in a circle. One. Two. Three.

Puffs of smoke come up from the middle of the stage like a simmering volcano that's been told *no* all its life.

I want to go in.

A rustle comes from the ticket window above.

And I become a ghost.

My fingers ease from the door, and soon that door's how King left it. As I back up, the door opens, and my book falls from my sweatshirt. I grab it and scoot around the corner, then stand straight up against the building.

Did the book make a noise? I'm pretty sure it made a noise. I pat my pouch. Please, let me not've dropped anything else.

My breathing is heavy enough that King would notice.

I try to simmer it.

The ribboned feet of the V point above me. I point my foot. Imagine it in ribbons. I trace a V, a tree split in half.

"What are you doing?"

King's eyebrows poke down. Must've seen me.

My toes are still pointed. What am I doing? "Practicing."

His brow wrinkles. "Practicing what?"

I lift my head to the sign. "Dancing. What you think?"

He blinks. "I think you're crazy. Let's go. Where are your boots?"

I lean back against the wall with relief. He didn't see me looking through the door.

"Hello?" he says. "Where are your boots?"

I look around. They're not here.

"Someone took them?" He whips his head around.

A movement at my side tells me something, and I turn to the blanket mound I noticed earlier. I nod my head to it.

Part of the blanket is lifted at the corner, and I point to a toe of black leather. Mine.

King takes a giant step over. He stands tall and uses his foot to lift the corner of the blanket. That corner could use a lot of thread.

One of my boots slides out from the blanket—dirty

fingernails around the heel. Then the other boot. The fingernails linger—small and girl-like. I feel bad for her, but I need those boots. They're mine.

The plastic in my pocket crinkles, and I switch my boots with Dad's half of banana moon. Everything else still in my pocket. The pie retreats and the blanket folds back down to the dark.

I'm glad I didn't have to fight. I'm not sure I would've, but I'd never tell King. I settle the boots on my shoulder, put my book back in place, and follow King.

"Did you get the money?" I ask.

"Naturally."

"You have to do anything to get it?"

"Not today I don't." Then he turns around with a smile so big I want to capture it. "Next week."

My back tingles from my waist to my neck. "Does that mean we're not leaving? We're staying with the Winterfolk?"

"No. Just means we gotta stick around awhile. We'll find somewhere to stay."

I let go of his smile. "What are they making you do for money?"

"You know, rob a bank. Okay . . . two. We'll be set for life."

I smirk at him.

He leans into me. "Dance."

The word slaps me. "I thought you don't do that."

"Denise promised it's *real* dance. Hip-hop. My kind of

dance. Not with signs, and not in there. Not like last time. She knows I won't do that. She's singing backup at another club next week, and they need dancers." He points to himself and bumps his hips.

"Can I go?"

"No." He turns back around and walks.

"I could be your backup. Or a backup to the backup. No one would see me."

"No."

"I could clean after the show. Wouldn't it need cleaning? I'd do it for free. If I do a good job, maybe they'd ask me back, and pay."

King keeps walking.

"What am I supposed to do if you're gone and someone comes looking?"

King stops but doesn't turn. I knew that'd get him, and I feel guilty for just a second.

"He won't," he says.

"That's what you said before, so what if he does?"

"Your dad has a metal pipe."

"But he'd never—"

"What about you?" he asks.

I imagine the pipe in my hands, and I open them wide to let it drop. "I'd . . ."

"Use it. You'd use it. Say it. Promise."

I look at my hands—not sure they're real enough to do something like that, but that's not the answer he wants. "If I had no choice . . . if no one else could."

"Good." He walks fast again.

The boot against my back kicks me to keep up with him. "But what if it's not enough?"

Now's the time to tell him what I did. I should tell him.

"Then we'll be prepared. I've learned how to be prepared. You know we're standing on top of a city?" he asks.

"You mean *in* a city."

"No. On top. We're on top of the Underground. There's a whole city made of wood under us. Wood. Remember the three pigs? Their wolf was fire. Destroyed everything it could burn. What's beneath is what's left. They rebuilt up here with bricks and concrete so it wouldn't happen again. We're standing on top a ghost town."

"Why'd they have to leave?" I ask. "Why couldn't they fix what they had?"

"They lost so much they became visionary. Like me. Taking precautions. Leaving the ghosts behind. See, they understood wolves come in different forms—just because one is bad doesn't mean the opposite is better. Water can put out fire, but that doesn't make you its friend. Danger can come from anywhere, and they prepared. They built up high to protect them from that other wolf—the friend guaranteed to be foe one day—a flood."

My teeth grit. "How do you know all this?"

"It's where I stayed when I first came here. Snuck in after a tour and stayed. People left, but I didn't. They show people the good places, but they don't know all of them. Places you can hide for nearly forever."

He points to the *Underground Tour* sign above a doorway. "You'd think that's the only way in, but it's not. There are many ways in. Not many ways out, though. It's dark down there. Sometimes when the light'd shine in, I used to look around me and think—when those buildings burned, they learned something. They used it to make them stronger."

I step onto a metal grid in the sidewalk. "How dark?"

"Like the night. You're standing on top a skylight right now. See these grids all down the walk? Beneath, during the tours, the guides turn on bright lights one section at a time. When they're done with that section, they turn it off. Soon, the only bit a light comes from the stars shining through the glass and the grates. Rectangles of checkered light."

I look down through the grate. "Would I be able to see anyone from up here?"

"No, but they can see you. Someone could be watchin' you now."

I jump off the grate. "How many are down there?"

"Enough, but like I said, there are ways to keep protected."

His words crawl up through the help numbers marked on my arm. That dark part of King he's kept from me. "I want to see it."

"I ain't never going back down, and neither are you. Smoke and dust. Trapped in a basement. Like a collection of ash and skin on display. Might look like a toy town, but those walls want to keep on burning. You can feel it. Got to turn into a rat to live. Saw plenty of them in corners." He shakes his head. "That's why we stay up high in the trees. Snatch every bit of light. That's the way to be visionary. Gotta keep on finding the light. That's what we'll do." His fingers dance in the air and grab at the invisible.

So many people on the street, but we don't walk around none of them. King walks straight, and the crowd parts for him. He's talking now about dancing—about what he's going to do when he gets up on that stage—and I'm not going to see it. He'll be dancing while I'll be zipped somewhere with my own dark thinking. Waiting.

Unless I don't go back with King. Find my own bits of light. I could go where I wanted. Stay where I wanted. He's already off in his own world. Look at him.

King steps off the curb—still talking—when a bus comes. Like the one that brought us here. King doesn't see. And it's going to smash him.

The bus driver's face is big in the window. Too late for him to do anything.

I grab King's arm and yank back hard. So hard we fall backward.

King's hair dances in the whoosh from the bus.

And we fall back—away from the street where the cars keep going and going, not even knowing what almost happened. What could've happened. If it hadn't been for me.

We're sitting now. Just sitting. One of King's legs crossed

over both of mine like we don't know which one of us saved who. His leg shakes, or is it mine, and he rubs his hands together, blows air in his hands. Proof the air's still in him. My heart booms. Drum music.

"You're not hurt," I say.

He shakes his head. Blows more air in his hands.

"My mom. She thought I had good reflexes," I say. "Only I don't remember her saying that. Dad told me. We were on the beach throwing a ball and she said, *Rain, I haven't ever seen anyone with reflexes like you*. Didn't know I still had them. Wonder what else my reflexes are good for."

King stands now, but I'm still in jitters.

"I guess for metal pipes," I say.

King pulls me to my feet.

"Want me to lead?" I adjust my book securely under my shirt while he looks off where the bus went.

He's shook up like I've never seen.

"Remember that game?" I ask. "The one we played when we were kids, King Says? I'll lead and you can tell me *King says walk straight*, or *King says turn right*, or you can trick me and say *Turn*. If I get it wrong, you take the lead again. What you think?"

His pupils glow like animal eyeshine. Must've gotten it from under the ground.

"King says the light is green," he says. "Walk."

And just like that I'm the leader.

8

I'M FLESH AND BONE with muscles and reflexes. I saved King. Couldn't save him if I'd been a ghost. Can't do much of anything if you're a ghost.

"King says keep walking."

Woulda had to tell Denise he couldn't dance for her. Her volcano would explode, and I'd have to take his place and dance on top a V cuz I wouldn't know how to get back home.

"King says stay straight."

Then I'd remember King saying I ain't that kinda girl, and I'd find a secret door to the Underground, where I'd become a rat and look at the stars through a grate. Poor Dad would sink in the earth and wouldn't be able to climb out again.

"Right."

He's trying to trick me, since he didn't say *King says*, but I want to stay the lead. I keep straight even though the cement ends ahead and cars are on the street. Nothing's in my way of seeing. I know he won't let me walk into the street.

"King says right."

I turn right. And smile. I knew he'd give in.

"Tired of surprises yet?" he asks.

"No. What is Denise like? Is she a good dancer? Does she have a lot of money? If I made money of my own, I could decide how to spend it. Right?"

"Right? I mean—King says keep straight. You want to know what it's like to be stuffed with money?"

"Sounds good to me."

"We'll go see Rachel. She'll tell you."

"You're going to let me talk to someone? In person?"

"Well, I don't got a phone to call her," he says.

Phone.

If I had a phone, I could call Matisse. I could give the bag back to her. I can do it. I can get Cook to leave us alone, and King wouldn't have to do a thing. I remember about phones being on street corners. I stop to look around but don't find any.

"What are you looking for?" He looks around as I did. "Did you see something? Maybe we shouldn't be here."

I shake my head and walk ahead of him again. "No, nothing. Come on. I want to meet Rachel. Maybe she has a phone. She must be a good friend if you're letting me talk to her."

"Ain't been too friendly to me. Kind of a pig, actually."

"Why we want to see someone like that?"

"Cuz she's loaded. Isn't that what you're after? Why do you want a phone?"

"No reason." My back tingles from talking to King, since I can't see him and he can see me. Shouldn't be that way if I'm in the lead, should it? I should be able to see everything.

"This here's Rachel. Go on and talk."

"She's a pig."

"I told you," he says.

So many people. More than I've ever seen. So many I can't tell one from the other. A mass of swinging arms and legs swirl around as we stand in the center of the market. I crowd close to Rachel and hug myself. Glad King can't see the goose bumps crawling up through the numbers under my long sleeve.

"You think I can talk pig?" I ask.

Someone bumps into me. I huddle closer to Rachel and rub my arms. "She's not even a real one."

King reaches out—to shove the person maybe, but he misses by inches. Too late. He shakes out his hands. "She's the size of a real pig. Bronze, too."

I hold my arms closer.

"Are you cold?"

"No." I focus on the pig. Easier than all this talking and shouting and music and honking and laughing and movement. So much movement. I focus on Rachel. "My hair's still wet, that's all. You said she's loaded?"

"Naturally. Come closer. Take a look." He points to a slot on the bronze pig's back. "People put money in there. There's thousands."

I put my eye to the slot, but Rachel's not showing me anything but the dark. That's fine with me. I'd rather be in the dark right now. "What they put money in there for?"

"Poor people. Do you wanna sit on her?"

I pull away. "Why?"

"I don't know. Sometimes I see people sitting on her and taking pictures. Guess they like riding pigs that keep quiet. That's what she gets. Put money in the pig, take a picture. Sometimes kiss her snout. Want to?"

"No."

"I'll put in a quarter."

"Go ahead and put in the quarter. I'm still not riding her or kissing her snout."

King digs out a quarter and drops it in. "For poor people." No hollow clink. Pig's probably half full.

"Can I have a quarter?"

"Why? You changed your mind?"

"No, it's not for Rachel. It's for me. In case I need it. I promise not to turn into a pig if you give it to me."

He lifts his eyebrows. "You mad?"

"No, but I figure if you're throwing quarters in a pig, maybe you could throw me one, too."

He keeps his eyes on mine as he fishes in his pocket and plants a quarter in my palm.

I drop it in my pouch. "Thanks." Now all I need is a phone, and a way to slip away for five minutes.

"You're acting strange."

"I told you I need practice," I say. "This is Pike Place?" There must be a phone.

I scoot close to Rachel, and my leg grazes her cheek. I look around. Try to break up the mass into parts so I can make sense of things. The people don't all walk the same— some fast, some slow—most don't pay attention to anything, but others take pictures with their eyes, and some with cameras to remember later what things look like. If I had one, I wouldn't take pictures of the streets or the buildings. I'd take pictures of small things—like that orange flower petal that's almost falling from its center, or that dripping slice of peach, fresh cut and being offered up for tasting. My mouth waters. The pieces are easier to see than the wholes. The wholes smother everything. Including phones.

"Can I stand on top the pig?" I ask.

"I don't think she'd mind. She's used to that."

I swipe his arm, and he smiles.

He steadies me as I climb and balance on top of her.

Now I can see. The streets and shops go on forever. Fruits and vegetables, meat and fish, breads with yeast scents. Jewelry of all kinds except for Dad's bracelets—not today— clothes, pictures, and decoration-hang-type things. Phones?

No phones. But people—wanting and pointing and buying. I imagine Dad here. A normal person doing his normal selling. Without anyone knowing about me.

I dig my big toe in the slot of the pig. I don't want to kiss it, but its edges kiss me hard enough to tear the foot of my stocking. They don't. Behind me are cheers.

For me?

I turn to the back of people's heads—they're watching. I watch, too. A fish flies—no, is thrown—through the air: mouth open. Used to be in the ocean.

People's mouths open.

The fish slaps down in thick hands. Another cheer. Yay, for the fish to become someone's dish. First comes the white paper wrapping.

Change happens so fast.

My body feels numb, and I hold up a hand to make sure I can see it, but my hand blurs and my knees sway. King's hand goes to my ankle. I don't want to be here no more. I'd rather be in the dark. Inside Rachel.

And then there's King, standing up here, too.

"Hey, hey," he soothes. "Steady. Close your eyes."

And I close them.

"Keep them closed and count to thirty," he says.

I count out loud to my fast heartbeat.

"Slow down," he says.

"4 . . . 5 . . . 6 . . ."

"Slower," he says.

"7 . . . 8 . . . 9 . . ."

Then he's silent as I keep counting. Almost like he's disappeared, but I know he's still there. And I'm almost home again in my rock garden.

"13 . . . . 14 . . . . 15 . . . ."

If I pulled off my cap, I'd feel his breath on my hair and I could shut out everything. Would be him and me, and no one else. Making our own world as always. Real enough for both of us.

"20 . . . . . 21 . . . . . 22 . . . . ."

I put my hand on my cap and begin to lift it.

"23 . . . . . . 24 . . . . . . 25 . . . . . ."

And that's when I hear it.

Drum music.

Real drum music. Not like back at the V.

This music is clear and familiar, and it's louder than my counting. It is the same drum as at home.

I stop counting, and no one tells me to keep going.

King's still here. Isn't he?

"King?"

I open my eyes. There I am. Through his dark pupils.

"See," he says, "you haven't disappeared. Neither have I."

Another fish flies through the air. This one's mouth is closed. The drum continues, but the fish won't tell me where it is. I twist to find the music.

"You hear the drum?" I ask. "Can you hear it?"

"Naturally." He points to a street corner with a fruit-and-veggie shop crowded with people. The people shift their weight with the drum, and between the shifting, some of the bodies part to reveal a drum and a grizzled head.

"Hamlet?" I ask.

"That's him."

"What's he doing here?"

The drumming ends, and more gaps appear. Some people peer into a white plastic bucket. I know what's in that bucket, and what might be for sale.

"No!" I jump off the pig.

I run to that corner. So fast King can't grab me.

I slip between the people gaps—King too big to do that—and dart to the bucket of hamsters. I slide my head between two others, jab out my elbows to make space, and check the hands around me.

All empty.

Down in the bucket. I stick my hands in—count the pink noses and fluffy bodies, some piled on top of one another, others squirming, happy to see me. Eleven.

I count again.

Eleven.

I count again.

There should be twelve.

Hamlet sits above on an upturned bucket. He's huge and gray from head to toe, practically stone. He's counting, too. Counting money while people wander off.

My face heats up.

When King shows at my side, Hamlet stands and glares.

King stuffs his hands in his blazer pockets and sniffs. Almost snarls.

"Looking to get attention?" Hamlet says. He nods toward me without looking.

I count the hamsters again and keep small.

"We won't be around much longer," King says. "And, it's her birthday."

I count again. Eleven.

"I know. I dropped a hamster off this morning. Traded with her dad."

Hamster twelve. From Dad?

I wonder what that hamster's doing. Probably sleeping like I'd be now. I want to see it.

A man in a green apron comes over with a full brown paper bag and hands it to Hamlet. The man goes back to his fruit-and-veggie shop surrounded by the same people who were listening to Hamlet's music.

Hamlet reaches in and pulls out two apples. Pink Lady—light shade of pink with yellow-green spots. They were Mom's favorite.

Hamlet gives them to King. "Feed her and take her back."

"Feed me?" I ask. "I'm not a hamster."

King shakes his head at me.

I shake my head back. "What? I'm not."

"Show her how they dance, first," King says. "She's never seen. After this, we'll go back."

Hamlet looks at me sideways—my hands still in the bucket—and he sits.

His drum is crosshatched all around in bamboo and stands taller than his lap. He cradles it between his knees and then brushes his fingers across the drum to set a quiet beat. A hamster moves beneath my hand.

They all do.

Hamlet uses his palm, and the sound gets bigger. The hamsters wiggle. People laugh and point at them.

I back away from their voices:

"Do you see them dancing?"

"They're not dancing. They're trying to get away from each other."

"They are dancing!"

"I'd go crazy trapped in that bucket."

"Ooh, gross."

Hamlet looks right at me.

Go.

9

"WHAT DID YOU THINK of their dancing?" King
points ahead to a hill of grass, and we walk that way.

"Did Hamlet train them, or did they already know?"

"What do you think?"

"I think they knew on their own."

He hands me an apple. "Sure. Why not."

I take a bite and catch the sugary juice before it drips down
my thumb. "Is that where you got your moves?"

He laughs and takes a bite of his own. "No. They got their
moves from me."

Something odd about King eating that apple. I can't figure it out.

He notices how I stare. "What?"

And then I know. "How come you're eating your apple that way? Why don't you use your blade?"

He shrugs. "It's dirty."

I swallow an apple lump. "Can't be that bad if he's following us."

He walks up the hill of grass. When we get to the top, the ocean comes to view, and my breath catches.

Only three or four streets lined with buildings down the other side of the steep hill separate us from the ocean. But there are no sandy beaches. Wooden docks line the shore, one after another, and drop to the water.

King watches me as he sits on the grass.

The ocean is bigger than I thought it'd be, and I know it's not *the* ocean. It's the Puget Sound, which leads to the ocean. Even so. It's big. And looks like the mirrored top of a puddle when the wind blows across to make ripples. But deeper and colder.

Too deep for swimming. Definitely too deep. But this is a safe distance. I drop my shoes to the grass and sit.

King turns his gaze to the water. His eyes narrow. Thinking, I guess.

I know patience.

I flex my feet to stretch my calves, tight with ache, and run my hand over the grass tips. They can't decide whether to tickle or prick me.

He finishes his apple in two more bites and places the core in the grass, where it hides.

I can't eat any more cuz of my stomach churning, but I don't want to set my apple down to get dirty. I hold it in the air and look around for something to wrap it.

"Use the washcloth." King fishes in my pocket before I can stop him.

He pulls out the baggie of white powder.

Seconds.

Less than seconds.

He looks at it.

He stabs it back in my pocket. "What the *hell*? What the hell, Rain?" he whispers loud. He's almost on top of me. "Where did you get that?"

And I let it all loose. "It's his. I'm sorry. He's not following you—it's me. I thought it would help us, and I wanted to take something of his. I really did. I wanted him to know how it feels to have something taken."

He backs off me, and I slip out from under him.

"How did you get it?"

I lift my sleeve to show the name and the phone number.

"Matisse?" he asks.

"She understands. I think she knows what he did to me."

He grabs my arm. "Do you know how stupid—"

"I know."

"If you got caught, you know they can take you away, right? You're a minor. And your dad isn't—"

"I know all that."

He lets go of me and takes a deep breath. "So . . . at the

library. You already knew he took your boots. And you were asking me all those questions?"

I can't look at him. I find the washcloth in my pocket, wrap the apple up tight, and fold it back in there.

"I can't believe you." He yanks my sleeve back down.

My eyes sting.

Since he searched in my pocket, I stick my hand in his. For the blade. But he grabs my wrist.

"I'm not the only one who did something stupid," I say. "Just for boots."

"You know it wasn't about boots." He lets go of my wrist. "I thought . . . I really thought I killed him this time. I wanted to."

I grab a fist of grass by its roots. And I hang on.

King pulls off his cap and drops it between his knees. He runs his hands through his hair. "Okay. We've just gotta think of a plan. It's gonna be okay."

"How do you know?" I feel for the locket beneath my shirt.

He touches the locket with a finger. "Ever try to open that?"

"It's glued."

"How do you know your mom's in there?"

"Cuz you told me."

"Like I'm telling you now. It's gonna be okay." He stands and pulls on his cap, then holds out his hand to help me up. "Come on. You have that girl's number, right? Matisse? I'll show you the waterfront—our edge, as far as we go. Then we'll call her, head back, and you can see your hamster. It'll all be over."

"All over." I let him pull me up. "And then we pack, and leave. While my trees get demolished, and the Winterfolk disappear like they never existed."

He keeps one hand on my arm. Doesn't answer.

I look past him to the ocean. "Looks cold, doesn't it? Too cold for swimming."

"Unless you're half fish." He smiles, but I can't.

"My mom swam in water like this."

"We can go back now if you want," he says. "We don't have to go out to the water."

"No. I want to see it closer."

He leads me through the indoor part of the market with an overhead sign. Has a hand with a finger pointing to the words: *More Shops*. Didn't think it needed more.

The shopwindows show what to expect, so people don't get disappointed. One is a bookstore with regular-type books, and another with comics. There's a whole store just for maps, and a small one, not much bigger than the doorway, for magic. And one's all dark with glowing stars. Fake stars. Imposters.

Each time we pass a shop, I pretend to visit a new country. I'll take anywhere but here, walking with King to the edge.

Here's a place with bronze goddess statues and long brown sticks with spicy smoke lifting from the tips. "India." We could stay the night. Wake up with that perfume in my clothes and hair and ride an elephant to the Taj Mahal. Then rise with the smoke and forget everything.

The next store is full of purple lavender—candles, wreathes, and lotions. "France," I say. "We'll climb the stairs to the top of the Eiffel Tower. I'll look down and won't be scared of falling."

King raises his eyebrows like I'm losing my mind, but doesn't say anything.

The next shop is wines. I know what wine looks like. Finished a bottle once after Dad fell asleep. I liked the taste even if it was bitter, but the wine got wasted when it came back through my mouth and nostrils outside the tent. Tried to keep quiet. I declare this is Italy, and forbidden for now.

We walk on ramps that lead us down. And down more ramps.

I yawn only because I'd be napping by now, and I'm running out of countries I know, and I'm so tired there's no use wanting anything more. "Is this a passage to the Underground?"

"If it is, I don't know it."

Then King looks over his shoulder, but not at me. I look behind, too, but don't see anything. King walks fast ahead. His hands fidget like they can't find anyplace to rest. In and out of his pockets, pulling at his cuffs, fingers wide and tense. He winds down a twisted, narrow hall, and he's faster.

I run halfway to get to him, stepping into something wet and sticky through my stockings. I cough not to gag.

He takes my hand, and we walk quick down some stairs that want to trip me, especially if I look straight down and don't see the one ahead. He opens the door to a stairwell, and we climb down some more. This time I do trip, but he catches me in time and we keep going.

I try to control my breath. "Are we running?"

"We might be."

My stockings keep sticking to the cement. Might be time to put on my boots, but King has them. I don't like having sticky feet, and I don't like having to run when I'm not running *to* anything. Had to run once with Dad, when someone thought I wasn't his—even when I screamed as loud as I could that I was.

I can scream loud when I want to.

"How did he find us?" I ask.

"I don't know." King pulls me around a corner, and I hold his hand extra tight while he looks around the wall at the stairs. He drops my boots and puts that hand in his pocket where his blade is. The wall's hard against the back of my head, and I knock my head on it a couple times to stop thinking.

"Please don't," I say.

I wish we were back in the laundry eating a MoonPie with my boots on my feet and King eating an apple with his blade.

"Your boots," he says.

I step in one to put it on.

"No." He bends down quick and grabs the other. He hurls it. But nothing happens. He scoops the other off my foot, but doesn't throw it. He takes my hand again, and I don't have time to look behind me at what he did. He opens the door, and I blink at the sun on the street. We run across, and down another, and the ocean's coming at me and getting bigger down the wooden pier. Cold and dark. My book clings to me.

Down the pier is the edge of land and water.

I look behind. I do and I see.

Cook.

Not hurt at all. Not one bit. Not that I can see.

The sun sparks off something shiny in his hand. A knife.

We keep running. Down a gray wooden dock like the one in my book. To the edge. Why are we running to the edge?

I tug my hand from King, but he holds on tight and pulls, and I've gotta keep up not to fall. The sound of good shoes thumps the wood behind us. A sliver of wood slices my foot, and I don't want to look. At the edge.

At the edge.

I close my eyes.

King lets go of my hand. His hand goes to my pouch.

But I hold it closed.

Someone pushes me.

I fall.

The cold, the wet, explodes, then:

Hushes

And takes my book of tales.

I open my eyes and the book floats up—the mermaid cover. I've read that book a zillion times and seen her swim. I take off my cap, and my hair swirls around me. I know this place. I've been here before. From the past. Or in one of my dreams.

I seal my legs together and dive down. I can swim. I can. I try to breathe beneath the water and harden myself to the freeze.

Bubbles squeeze from my mouth, and my chest presses in. I'm near the bottom. There is a bottom. Mom? Is she down here? No. But one of her rocks is.

I can't breathe.

I grab for the rock. But its wish is so big it would take three people to lift.

Did you fall from the sky?

Were you a star?

More bubbles from my mouth. Bigger ones.

I can't.

I can't breathe.

The water's hands are all around me—at my throat, lungs.

I'm not a mermaid.

I can't swim.

I look up. A shadow. A person. Swims toward me.

I'm in King's Underground, and there's no more light.

10

KING? IT'S TOO DARK. You said we could see the stars through the grate, but I can't. The stars smell salty. I taste them on my lips. I remember now. I kissed them to sleep, and they kissed back.

Whispers in the dark. Whispers.

And a pinpoint of light.

The wind whispers across the water, and the light gets bigger—a glow larger than a flame, and larger than a grate.

Someone sets me down on a dry surface. Beneath my fingers, my palms. Splintered wood.

"Do you remember?" someone says. "Do you remember?"

My head throbs, and I don't want to remember. The light

hurts my eyes, and I squeeze them shut. I'm too cold. Can't move my arms. Can't move my legs. A choke of air escapes me.

Something is wrong.

That string on the tent must've come undone and torn down the middle. Tears have rained down on me. A whole ocean of tears. My clothes are heavy with trouble pressing me down. Always pressing. A blanket covers me, but it's not my blanket, not Dad's.

"I saved her."

Daddy didn't save her.

"I saved her."

Not King.

"You did an okay job, squirt. Holding her leg. I was on pure automatic, man."

A deep voice. "You're both heroic."

"I did more than hold her leg. I saved her book, see?"

"You mean what's left of it."

"It's important. It's a library book. Do you think they'll make her pay for the damage?"

Deep voice. "I'm sure something can be worked out. After all, it's not her fault."

"Maybe when it dries it will be like new again. She looks like the mermaid on this cover. Do you think she is?"

A mermaid.

"Let me see the book."

"No! *I'm* giving it to her. I saved it."

"I just want to see it."

Deep voice again. "She's opening her eyes."

Three heads—one big, one medium, one small—the three bears.

"What's your name?" says the baby bear.

I try to lift my head, but it wonks back down.

Papa Bear wears a cap. "Easy there. You've had a bit of an accident. Just rest a minute before trying to move."

Mama Bear's not a mama. She's a boy about my age with blond hair. Not Cook. And he's wrapped in a brown blanket. He pushes his head in. "I saved you."

Baby Bear smiles shy. Also in a brown blanket. "Are you a mermaid?"

I wiggle my toes.

Am I?

The older boy pokes him with his elbow. "Of course she's not."

The small one holds out my book. "Look what I saved for you. Do you want it?"

I can't help but grab it and hold it to me.

"See?" gloats the little one. "I told you she'd want it."

"Miss?" says Papa. Papa in dark blue.

I blink the water from my eyes. He's police.

I scramble back, the blanket falls from me, and he grabs my upper arm. I freeze solid while the edges of me drip. Around me are more and more people.

People can see me.

I'm not a mermaid, and I'm not a ghost. I'm a hamster. I'm one of Hamlet's hamsters, and they want me to dance.

I hold to my pouch. Look around for King.

"Hey, careful, careful," Police says. "You're in shock, I know, but no one's going to hurt you. You're safe. He's gone."

Gone.

I search around me. King?

"Move back, boys," says a woman's face. If I touched her cheeks, they'd be soft.

The older boy rolls his eyes. "Mom, I've trained for this."

The woman smiles a close-lipped smile at me, careful not to bare teeth.

Police puts the blanket back over me—more scratchy than the one in my tent. Must be new and never been washed. I need to get my laundry. Go get my laundry and go home. I need to get my laundry.

Police looks in my eyes but not like King does in his smooth way when he wants answers. Police digs. "Do you know him? We're looking right now, and got a good description from these two."

The older boy throws off his blanket and scoots forward. "He was black or Indian or whatever, had a black velvet blazer and a skullcap with a cross on it. He pushed you in the water and then ran off."

King pushed.

Police clears his throat and signals the older boy to move

back, which he does. "Yes, very helpful. Do you know him?"

King pushed me.

"Okay, that's fine. That's fine. I'm sure we'll find him. Don't worry. Can you tell me your name?"

Sirens blare in the background. Behind the crowd is Police's car with red-and-blue flashing power lights. Do they know about the baggie? I grab the front of my pouch, which crinkles.

"Your name?" he asks again.

The little one inches up with his blanket and puts his hand on his chest. "My name is Doryn." He holds his hand to me. "Your name is . . ."

"Doryn," I repeat.

"No," he says with patience. "Doryn is *my* name. *Your* name is . . ."

"She's in shock," the older one says. "Lifeguard training."

"I thought she might not speak English."

The older one purses his lips and squints at me. "Me llamo Carter. ¿Cómo te llamas?" He looks back at Doryn. "See? Nada. She's in shock."

"We need to get ahold of her parents," Police says. "Did you say that's a library book?"

Doryn nods. "The stamp says Beacon Hill."

"Then she's probably not a tourist. She's local. The library should have a record of who she is along with an address. You stay here with her. I'll go make a call."

The moment he lets go of my arm, I'm up and running

through the biggest gaps. Tips of fingers try to grasp, but that's all they are. Tips because I'm so fast, and I try to remember how to be a ghost again.

"Wait!" Police calls with his black shoes running after me.

"Mermaid!" shouts Doryn.

King pushed me.

Run. Keep running. Doesn't matter where. My body will take me. My wet stockinged feet slap the cement and leave a trail. I run on my toes to make the marks as small as a cat's. I've got to take my stockings off to not leave a trail, but I don't have time. I've got to run. I can't hear anything but my feet. I can't see anything but the spaces in front of me. My side cramps, and I use my book to hold it in and keep running.

Drum music. Tinny radio drums.

I look up. Red-ribboned ankles atop a big blue V.

My feet led me here, and now they're on fire and my legs are going to melt. I can feel it. They're gonna. They're starting. I stumble to the blanket mound still against the wall—and sink. My legs burn and melt, and I hide behind the mound to watch for Police. Try to keep still.

I curl in a ball and shrink closer to the mound. I stick my toes beneath the blanket. Scoot in half a foot. A whole foot.

The blanket lifts. And covers me.

11

"YOU'RE DELICIOUSLY WET."

This is not a girl. A boy with a fairy tale face and white mohawk hair.

"Don't worry, I'm not a perv," he says.

"A what?"

"I won't molest you. I just want to . . ." He scoots closer. He's slightly bigger than me, but just as thin.

I grip the blanket, ready to escape if I need to.

He lowers his long-lashed eyes and bows his head. He rests his brow on my wet shoulder. "Ah, that feels good. It's so hot in here. Calm down. You're making me queasy." He turns his head to get at his cheek.

I glance at his red-white-blue plaid. "Are you wearing a skirt?"

"It's a kilt. Why are you so wet?"

Then I remember. "The trail."

He hums prettily.

"I think I left a wet trail from my feet. Someone's chasing. Police."

He pops up from my shoulder and peers out the blanket. "I don't see anything."

"No trail?"

"No."

I feel the sore bottoms of my feet. The tops are wet, but the bottoms are dry from all my running. My finger bumps against a splinter. "Ow." I prop up my foot to get a better look and manage to pull it out.

"Oh." He shuts the blanket back up. "Cop car."

I hug in my knees.

"Chill. They won't see us. What did you do? Steal pennies from a fountain? Don't think I haven't thought of it."

I start counting to thirty in my head to relax. The hot air stifles. I drape my wet sleeve on my face and the coolness releases me.

"I could use some of that quenching," he says, "if you want to stay under here."

I hand him my wet hair, and he holds it to his face.

My cap. I don't have my cap to hide my hair. Oh, well. Something tells me even a cap couldn't hide who I am.

"You smell like the ocean." He runs my hair over his rosy, chapped lips. "It *is* the ocean."

My cap must be in the ocean. Where King pushed me. "I fell."

"You're sure? You don't sound sure. Where's your fine friend?"

My hair slips from his fingers as I turn to him. "You saw us? From before? You watched us the whole time, didn't you? And you stole my boots." Rubber bands hold the toes of his shoes together, but it's no excuse.

"You abandoned the poor things." He takes my hair again and squeezes water to his palm. Cautious. "Where are your boots? They looked too big for you."

"If you're so hot, why do you stay under here?"

He pats the water on his neck. "I was trying to sleep. Day's the only time to do it, you know, and I can't sleep when people can watch me. Not that they would. But they could. There's always the occasional jerk."

"Why can you only sleep in the day?"

His green eyes sparkle like my soon-to-be cat's. "You don't know? Where do you live?"

I swallow. "That's a personally question."

"A personally question." He tickles his chin with the ends of my hair. "Personally, I live here. Now you."

"Personally. I, uh . . ."

"Do you live with your friend? What are you—thirteen, fourteen?"

"Fifteen."

He raises a doubting eyebrow. "And you live with him?"

"Not all the way together."

He crooks his head. "But, near each other."

I swallow again.

"Sweet Mary, you live in the Jungle!"

I grab my hair from him and try to laugh. "I do not."

His eyes weigh me. "You do. I know your friend. Well, I don't know him, but I know *of* him, and one of the things I know is he lives in the Jungle. He *is* the Jungle. No one in their queerest of minds would live there unless you have protection. That, or you have one boner of a death wish." He chews at his chapped bottom lip. "Where is he? Will he come here looking for you?"

I hug my book and bite at my longest fingernail, which has turned to a salty fish scale. "I dunno. We were supposed to meet . . . somewhere if anything bad happened, but I can't go there anymore. Not yet. And I dunno if he still wants me."

He raises both eyebrows. "Wants you?"

"Never mind. I need to get home. I need to get my laundry and go home. Can you show me how to get back there?"

"Hell, no. I want to live."

"No one will care if you're with me. They know me. My dad will be waiting, and I don't know what he'll be thinking. And I don't know what's happened to King. He might need help. I need to go."

"You live with your dad? He lets you live there?"

"I . . . we have a nice place. We've had it for a long time. It has a rock garden. And we have neighbors."

Hamlet.

"Hamlet can take me back home! He's at the market. I can get him." I stick my legs out of the blanket.

"I thought the police were after you. Or your friend. Or whatever."

I tuck my legs back in. "Please help me. I don't care about the laundry no more. I just need to get home."

He chews at his lip again. "What does Hamlet look like?"

"Grayish. He plays a drum at the market. His hamsters dance."

"Oh, that guy. The one who puts a vibrator under the bucket. Creative use, I must say."

"A what?"

He sighs. "Suppose I look for your Hamlet. And you stay here with my blanket. How do I know you won't take it?"

"I don't take stuff."

"But I don't know you. What can you give me to make sure you don't take my things?"

"Your things? You mean your blanket?"

"Yes, my blanket. It's been with me a long time. What can you give me, and don't say your book. I don't want your soggy book." His eyes move to the gold beaded chain at my neck.

"How about my name?"

He leans forward, his face a thumb's length away. "Your real one."

I stare back. The way I've seen King do. "Rain."

He laughs and takes my hair in his fists. The water trickles to the ground. "Of course. What else could it be?"

I don't know if he believes, so I keep staring.

"All right, Rain. I'll be back." Like that he's disappeared. Then he pokes in his head. "I'm Jessiebel."

"Jessiebel."

He nods. "Jessiebel, the conniving slut."

Then he's really disappeared.

I suck on my hair at all my never thoughts. Never thought the ocean would be salty as tears. Never thought I couldn't swim. Never thought King would hurt me.

Maybe it's the fish that are doing all the crying, or the mammals that live there—giant whales with giant tears. I pet the mermaid on the cover of my book and turn to the last page, where she's turned into air. The tears could be hers. Who could wait so long in silence?

I remember the baggie and stick my hand in my pouch to feel for it. Still there.

Heels spike-click out of the V—right up close to me—and I tense.

"Jess." A woman's voice. Fake sweet. Denise?

I sit up tall. *Don't ask me to leave.* I won't leave. I'd rather dance than leave.

"There's my little chicken. I have a refreshment for you."

I shrink. *Little chicken.* A bottle clinks to the ground next to my feet.

"We have a party coming. Clean up in the bathroom. If we need you, you can sleep in the back tonight. Be perky."

I nod.

The heels spike-click back in.

Little chicken. I open my book to the sea witch surrounded by her serpents, then slam it shut.

With a single finger I lift a corner of the blanket. Not a serpent. Not poison. Only beer. I'm overthinking because I'm overthirsty. I'm losing my mind to tales. I lick my salt lips. Just a sip would be okay. The bottle's colder than my hand, but a nice sorta cold. My whole body knows it's going to get something. My mouth waters.

I put the bottle to my lips and tip in the gold liquid. It's like drinking bread. I swallow again, then pry the bottle from my lips. My stomach growls angry.

Oh, Jessiebel. You'd better come soon, or you won't have no more beer. My stomach is greedy. I shouldn't've given it so much today—making it think it could be so big with all that MoonPie and chili. It hurts when it gives up space— like there's a war going on with my stomach always losing. It wants too much. The cramp comes on again, and I can't help but take another sip since it will stop my stomach from shrinking.

How am I supposed to feed a cat? Or my new hamster.

King will help.

King pushed me.

I take another drink. He didn't mean to. He wouldn't.

And that's how they find me—

With the bottle to my lips

Drinking

The last of the sips.

With my forehead gone tingly, and my mind soft on King.

About what might've happened if we hadn't run to the edge.

Cook had a knife. We were trapped. He wanted me.

And then I understand.

King got me out of the way.

He didn't push me.

He saved me.

"Was that my beer?" Jessiebel taps his toe—the loose sole wags at me with a foul odor.

I extract my tongue from the bottle and laugh at the wagging mouth. Until I see Hamlet.

Giant and gray. Not saying a thing.

With his apples, his drum, and his bucket of hamsters.

I bite the edge of the bottle. "Denise says you have a job. To wash up and maybe sleep out back. What kinda job is it you getta sleep at night?"

"Nothing King wouldn't know." He takes the empty bottle from me as if it still has worth.

"Come," says Hamlet.

I stand and turn to Jessiebel. "She called you her little chicken."

"That's what she calls all of us."

"So you can't go in there." I lower my voice. "She's a witch."

He laughs. "Your first beer? Nothing's wrong with listening to some music and moving with the other little chicks." He drops his palm on Hamlet's drum and thumps it.

Hamlet shoves the bag of apples at me and grabs Jessiebel's wrist. Jessiebel squirms to wrench it away, but Hamlet's strong.

I squeeze the bag against me. "You shouldn't've done that."

"No shit. I'm sorry, okay? What is it with guys and wrists? Is it a daddy thing?"

Hamlet throws down his wrist.

Jessiebel rubs at it. "This is what I get for helping you? An empty bottle and a twisted wrist? How about that necklace, huh?"

I squeeze the bag harder to guard me. Hamlet reaches into it and holds an apple out to Jessiebel.

I remember the half-eaten one in my pocket, salt marinated, and think of Dad. Wonder if it'll make him sick to taste the ocean.

"Keep it." Jessiebel picks his blanket off the ground. "I'm going to have a feast tonight. Eat food straight out of your dreams, and I don't want to spoil my appetite. Tell King he owes me for my assistance. He'll know how to pay properly. Now, if you'll excuse me . . ."

Hamlet steps aside, and Jessiebel disappears through the lair.

"Have you seen King?" I ask Hamlet.

"Come."

12

ALL THE HAMSTERS ARE asleep, and I'm as floaty as they are—only a twitch of the ear here and there when the bus hits a bump. I wonder if they dance in their dreams, if they rear up to dance in pairs—boy-girl, boy-girl, boy-girl, boy-boy, girl-girl, and one lonely boy since his partner's back home.

I'll dance with you, I tell him. *You can dream about me.*

I don't feel anything hidden at the bottom of the bucket. Jessiebel was so wrong. They dance lovely.

I shiver as cold air blows through slits at the top of the bus. My damp sweatshirt's chilly and leaves wet spots on my seat. Can't wipe it with anything. Driver didn't even look when I climbed on after Hamlet. All he saw was money going into the machine.

The bus hits another big bump, but I hang on to the doubled-up buckets—one for the hamsters and the other for Hamlet's stool when he plays his drum. Nearly all Hamlet's world is here on this bench. The brown bag of apples crinkles in his big hands over his drum as the bus turns. It's a good thing I'm holding the bucket instead of him holding it. I can keep the hamsters steady and gently dreaming. They're going home, and I'm going home. I do want to go home. Really.

The hamsters nuzzle against one another.

Boy-girl, boy-girl. Soon I'll see King.

"I was saved twice today," I say.

Hamlet doesn't move.

"Into the ocean and out of the ocean. That's how love happens in stories. When you get saved. Or you save him. Those three who pulled me out—the little one was sweet, but he was too little. Mama Bear, Papa Bear, Baby Bear. None of them were just right."

The bus bounces again.

"But King saved me, too. When he pushed me in."

"He left you. I'll deal with him."

"He didn't have a choice. You're not listening. Someone was chasing us. Someone dangerous."

His head jerks. He checks around. The nearest person's a few seats away. "*You* are the one who's dangerous."

I laugh. "Me?"

"All this running around. Bringing attention. You're why

we got those notices."

"No, it's not. No one's seen me."

"Like today?" he asks.

"Today's different. I'm not the reason."

"Aren't the police looking for you? That kid with the mohawk said so."

"Yes, but to help—"

"A helpless young thing like you." His face crinkles. Might even crack.

I look out the windows over Hamlet. "That's not fair."

"No," he says. "It's not."

I don't recognize anything familiar outside, and my head fights against the fog caused by the beer. "Where are we?"

Hamlet clears his throat. "I never supported a child living with us. I told them this would happen."

I scoot to the edge of my seat and speak loud. "Where are we?"

"Lower your voice. They'll put you in a nice home with everything you need and leave the rest of us alone. Should've done this long ago."

I half rise, and the hamsters stir. "That has nothing to do with it. You can't take me from my family."

He looks at me hard. "You have no choice."

I stand in the aisle with the bucket hostage. "I'm not help-less."

He leans forward and slowly lifts his hand to me. "You've been a ghost for years. You don't speak. Sit back down."

I scream. Past the rising hurt in my throat. "Stop the bus!"
Hamlet's eyes widen, and the bus lurches as people stare.

They see us.
They see me.

And that's when I understand. Part of being seen is showing yourself.

He springs up, and I tip the white bucket to the ground.
The hamsters pile in a lump—black, brown, gray, orange,
white—boy-girl-boy-girl-and-lonesome-boy. They scatter
free across the floor as people shriek.

"Babies!" Hamlet drops to his knees. "Oh, babies!"

The doors of the bus open.

And the hamsters dance.

13

THE HIDING SPOTS ARE different here. The trees are too far apart, the rocks the size of pebbles. Narrow alley streets separate buildings—possible for hiding—but my head tugs me past them. Unsafe.

I notice the ones who think they're hiding. But I see them. They cling to corners where walls meet. Some eyes say *Occupied*. Some eyes are stuck in ghost worlds. Other eyes—his eyes, that one smoking a cigarette stub in clean clothes—are friendly. I take a step to him. A sharp rock jabs my heel.

He drops the stub and grinds it underfoot.

I take another step. What should I say? *Take me to the Jungle?*

He smiles.

Too friendly.

He'd hide me. For sure.

"Winterfolk."

Who said that? I turn to a woman who's looking down at the sidewalk.

Reading.

I read, too, and that's what it says.

WINTERFOLK

It's Matisse's writing.

But why?

"Winterfolk," I say.

The woman looks at me. She's as old as my mom would be. She walks away.

I follow the woman, though I'm not sure the reason.

A suit jacket and skirt, her hair in a neat bun. She walks fast, but I keep up with her. She turns the corner ahead. I speed up not to lose her and catch her walking into a coffee shop.

Coffee. What did Matisse say?

I back up to look at the sign overhead. *Swallow.* No, not where Matisse works. She said *Spazz.*

I feel my sleeve. Still wet from the ocean.

Oh, no.

Matisse's number.

I tug up my sleeve and prepare to see smears from the water. Instead, there are solid, black numbers. I kiss my arm.

That lady moves up in line. I step closer to the window.

All those people right up close to one another, and they don't talk. They tap and wipe at phones.

Phones that can call numbers in black Sharpie.

All of them—except for the woman, who stares off into space. I wonder if she has a phone. I imagine my mom here. In line. Getting coffee. She'd stare off the same way as this woman.

The woman's eyes float around the room, they float out the window over me. She steps up to the counter and states her order. Exchanges money. Waits. I wait with her. She doesn't know I'm keeping her company.

I imagine where she's going next. To a building, an office with a big desk. She'll leave before it gets dark. Before the stars come out. Stop off at the store to get groceries, and when she gets home, she'll make dinner for her family. Spaghetti. She'll smile, and it'll be a real smile when she tucks them into bed. She'll unwrap that bun at the back of her head, unwind her hair down to her feet, and walk out the front door.

She turns to take the coffee.

I scoot from the window and lean up against the brick. The door opens, and I pretend not to look.

She holds out a cup to me.

She sips on one while she holds out the other. For me. She did see me.

I take it from her. "Thank you."

Her eyes disappear again, and I try to pull them back. "Do you have a phone—"

But she's gone.

I sit up against the wall and drink the coffee. Some help. Some people help.

I need to call Matisse. She said to call her. She'll help. She's already helping.

It's because of her I got this coffee.

I watch one after another walk out the shop. They all have phones. I could ask. I should ask.

One by one, they leave.

Now I really will ask—this guy coming out of the café in T-shirt and jeans. Old enough to be my dad, but this man's shirt doesn't have any wrinkles. He's walking away.

"Excuse me." I run up to him.

His head turns. He almost smiles, but then he glances at my stocking feet and walks away faster.

I'm quicker to the door this next time—two ladies in short summer dresses.

"May I use your phone?" I ask them.

They don't see me. They don't hear me. Except for one who rolls her eyes. She did see me. I know she did.

"Hello?" I say to her.

Too late. They're gone.

I throw away my cup.

Some people help. Some people don't.

I turn myself in a circle to see where I am. I'm on a hill. Farther up are buildings and more hills. I can't see the top. Down the hill—still more buildings, and I can't see the end of them.

This morning I sat on the wall with King and we looked down to the ocean. Down where my boots scattered near the shore. Down at my feet, a rip in my legging starts at my big toe up to my knee. I want my boots back. Which are down by the water.

Down, down, down.

I find the stairs. All by myself, I find them. When I saw the market, I knew where to go. I remembered everything. Strange how some memories stick to you, while others are hard to find. Some, you hold—try to feel their edges and figure out their shapes—sort out if it's yours or someone else's.

My feet are at the top of the stairs.

I check for people and step down quiet. The steps are nicer to me this time, maybe because I'm not trampling on them.

I imagine King at the bottom, picking up my boot, with the other in his hand. *Where you been?* I ask. He shrugs. *I been looking for you. What you think?*

Only that's not what happens when I get to the last stair. No one is there.

I look around for my boot. The concrete is spackled with hard gum and grime, and under the stairs is a small shadow.

I don't like shadows.

They lie. You can never tell what they really are until you're close up, when it's too late to do anything. I push away the curiosity of shadows. Most of the time.

I duck my head under the stairs and move closer.

The corner smells like urine. I cover my nose, and the shadow moves. A furry shadow—not a hamster kind of furry. A rat kind. Which turns its black eyes and sharp-bone feet to me.

I step back. Slow. I don't want it chasing.

Rats are Old World, King says. They have memory of rats before them. To be smarter than a rat, you have to turn into one. I had nightmares of them nibbling my hair when we didn't have food. King built traps. Does this rat remember? Was it the one I set free—fur matted with a clump missing on the hump of its back?

The rat's mouth opens.

I scuttle back.

A hand grabs my arm.

I look up into eyes. *Too friendly.* He smiles—

Bared teeth stained with nicotine.

14

"CAREFUL," HE SAYS.

I try to tug away, but his grip only gets tighter.

"Are you hungry?" he asks. "You look hungry."

"Let me go."

"What happened to your shoes?" A fat tongue licks his bottom lip.

I reach a hand in my front pocket and close it down on my bound apple.

"Do you need some shoes?" he asks. "Come with me. I'll get you some shoes. How did you get so wet?"

I turn my head away.

"You don't got to be afraid of me. I'm with the missionary." He smiles.

The rat twitches. Been around a long time. Doesn't believe this man's out for saving—any more than I do.

The man nudges my arm.

"What's that book you have there, sweetie?"

His stubby fingers reach out.

I hold it away.

He laughs like I'm teasing.

I'm not. My sharp fingernails dig into the apple.

He reaches for the book again.

Heat rises up in me. Heat and hate. And something else: Fight.

I swivel and throw my fisted apple in the rat's direction.

The rat takes the cue.

Its long tail drags behind, but it charges. And it knows me. I see that. It charges at the man, and the man's stubby fingers let me go.

I run as that man's eyes change to none too nice, and the rat scales up his leg. That man shouts all kinds of words. At me. At the rat. We're the same to him.

My heart thunders with my run, and all I hear is breath and heart, and heart and breath.

I run into the biggest open spaces with more and more people, who don't know they're helping. They only need to be here to keep that man away from me.

My feet transition from concrete to soft wood.

And I stop.

Look up.

With the ocean in front of me. And this time, it doesn't frighten. It's big, and I know how cold it is from how dark it is, but it's not endless. Across the way, in all directions, are islands covered in Evergreens. You would have to swim around them to get lost in the water.

If I follow the edge to the spot King left me, he could be waiting. He could.

A breeze covers me in salt and earth.

The smell of warm, fried food drifts to me, and my stomach barks back. Nothing likes to be teased.

It's fried food, I tell it. *Junk.*

But it forces my eyes to the restaurants on the pier with outside tables and chairs and people eating all kinds of things, and it doesn't look like junk at all.

One table has three chairs with two blond boys and a mom.

"Mermaid! Mom, look! It's the mermaid!"

Stupid fairy tale.

15

DON'T TURN. KEEP WALKING.

"She's not a mermaid," the older boy says. Carter. That's his name.

I'm not a mermaid.

The small one's shoes are too fast. The medium one's too greedy. The mama one . . . the mama one . . .

I hug my book. None of them are just right. Keep walking.

They've slowed now. Right behind. Walking as slow as me. The pier's edge ahead—where we all first met. The beginning is the end, and the end is the beginning. Except King's not here.

Their family of shoes stops as I keep walking.

And then I see it.

My boot—

Flipped on its side, tongue wide open. Laces spilled out in a tangle.

No one's taken it. No one would. Useless without its pair—how Dad tells me. We belong in pairs.

I kneel down to it. Touch the leather toe. Expect it to breathe. And there is breathing . . . behind me.

I put down my book, take the boot in my hands, and slip in my foot with the torn stocking. Pull the strings tight. Tighter. I remember what Mom taught me. Form a bunny hole. The bunny runs around the hole. Squeezes through.

Escapes.

Their footsteps come to me.

I bow my head, and my hair covers my face.

A hand touches my head, and my locket burns my heart. I know that hand is a woman's. Some things I remember. Some things I don't need my dad to tell me.

"We were wondering where you went," she says. "We just sat down to dinner. Would you like to join us? Do you like fish and chips?"

"Fish 'n' chips." I look up. Fish 'n' chips from King.

"She's talking!" Doryn says.

"She's repeating," Carter says, but his eyes hold interest.

Doryn squats beside me. "Fish and chips. And my favorite—clam chowder. Do you want some?"

Yes, my stomach says.

"Okay?" Doryn asks.

Yes. I want to eat.

The mom's hand moves from my head to my shoulder. To my arm. She pulls, and I go with her.

Food that doesn't come in a bag tastes different. Here, on a plate, I see all the fish 'n' chips at one time. Bags tease. Sometimes they hide a piece, and when you find it, you get a gift. Sometimes you think you have more, but you don't, and nothing can keep away the hollow in your stomach.

Food on a plate is simple. It says, *Eat me or don't. You decide.*

Okay, I will, I say, and I pick up a french fry.

I dip it in a cup that someone personally squeezed some ketchup in, and I swirl the fry. Dip, dip. I take my time. Even though my stomach grumbles.

The wind blows my hair from my face so I can eat.

And then I taste the salt. The sweet ketchup. The crisp, then hot, soft center. The ketchup leaves its prints on my fingers. I lick.

How about some fish? the plate says.

I pick up a medium piece and tear it in three bits. I dip one in tartar—the right amount to save some for each and every piece. And then I let it melt in my mouth.

A bowl of hot chowder waits for me. So warm in my hands. I tilt it to my lips.

A giggle stops me. Doryn, next to me. He's eating his chowder with a spoon. They're all eating with spoons.

Wasteful when you can sip from a cup. Carter and their mom are trying extra hard not to look, but Doryn smiles. A nice smile.

I set my bowl down and touch the handle of the silver spoon. Mom stirred sugar into her coffee with a silver spoon. I remember that. Can't do that with your finger unless you want to hurt yourself. That wasn't her intent.

Her spoon always made a sound—*clink-clink-clink*.

Clink.

Doryn spoons up his last bite.

I like looking at him. He's what a real kid should look like. He's miniature everything—blond like his family, but with a front tooth missing and a soft pink scar across the bottom of his chin. I wonder how he got it—climbing a tree, riding a bike, roller-skating, or pretending to be a plane. Running for the fun of it. I wonder if it hurt when he fell. I wonder if it was worth it.

He and Carter have changed their clothes. The salt is drying in mine, and it scratches.

I don't like looking at the mom. But hard not to. She has a trinity of moles on her forehead. I want to connect them with my ketchup into a triangle. I read about the Bermuda. I liked to think Mom swam there, got lost, and would find her way out.

Carter sneaks a peek at me—his eyes try to occupy mine. I know what he's thinking. *I saved you.*

I'm not yours, I tell him.

Carter wipes his mouth with a cloth napkin, sure to leave a cream smear on all that white.

Forks lift, knives cut. All around me—as if it's normal to eat outside with a fork and knife.

As if knives are only used for eating.

I wonder what King's knife looks like—for I'd rather think of that than what King might look like. As I'm here in a chair with food in my mouth. I know he fought. It's the only reason he'd leave me.

My stomach's had enough.

I fold my hands on my lap, on top my book.

"The sun will be setting soon," the mom says.

And then it will be too dark to find home. I used to like the dark, but now I don't want to look at the corners around me. What might be watching.

Is that King?

A black skullcap peeks out from across the street.

I stand, and my water cup knocks over. My book falls to the ground. Everyone else jumps up.

Where did he go?

People cross in and out every which way, and he's gone.

Couldn't have been King. He woulda stayed and let me see. He'd take me back. We'd go back together.

I keep standing.

"What is it?" the mom says.

Doryn wipes the water with a napkin.

I'm so clumsy. Shouldn't be at a table. I take my napkin

and try to help. "So sorry."

They all turn to me with big eyes. As if they heard my hamster—the one waiting for me—speak. No one expects creatures to have a voice. But they do.

Doryn whispers, "She talks English."

Of course I do.

Ice burns my hand when I pick it up off the tablecloth, but I let it burn. The only frozen water I've had is snow, with my face and hands cold. I set the ice on my hot tongue, and it melts easy. I try to find the flavor. Minerals, earth, season. King makes fun when I do it. But all water tastes different. I read once how we're mostly water, and I think when something's so much a part of you, it's hard for some to see a difference. But I can. This water's not from here.

Doryn picks my book off the ground. "Where's your other shoe?" he asks.

Gone. An accident. Or not an accident.

I bite the ice, which is almost melted now. Nearly gone.

I step out some more and look for King. My clothes move stiff against me.

"I need to get my laundry."

"What?" The mom comes over to me. "Your laundry?"

She must be tired of me. I bite the ice again and nod. If I can get to my laundry, I'm sure I can get home.

"I can call a cab for you. What's the laundromat called?"

"Coin Laundr. The *y* is missing."

"Coin Laundry." She rubs her palms over her mom hips.

"Do you know where it is? Do you have an address?"

Addresses again. I want to draw her a map with the library and good Hank's Hot Dogs & Chili and the laundry and the Jungle.

Instead, I point. I know it's in that direction.

She takes a phone from her purse and does some things to it. She has a phone. She squints her eyes and looks deep into the crystal ball part. "There are seventy-eight coin laundries in Seattle."

That's not so many.

She sighs. Too many. She's putting her phone away.

"It's by Hank's," I say. "Hank's Hot Dogs & Chili."

I wish the boys would stop staring at me. *YES, I CAN SPEAK.*

She frowns and does more things to her phone. Her head shakes. "I can't find a Hank's Hot Dogs & Chili."

"Used to be fish 'n' chips." I should tell her about the library, but I can't go there if they know about the book. I can tell her the place, though. "Beacon Hill. The laundry's in Beacon Hill."

She presses more buttons. "Now I'm getting eighty-three. Isn't Beacon Hill part of Seattle? It should be less than seventy-eight."

I'm sure there's only one with a *y* missing.

I pull up my sleeve. "Will you call this number?"

She pulls back. "On your arm? Oh. Well. Okay." She dials. "Why do you have a number on your arm?"

I don't think she needs an answer.

"It's ringing," she says.

We wait.

"Hi," she says. "Matisse? My name is Kerry and I'm here with . . ." She looks to me.

I shouldn't say my name.

She wrinkles her forehead, and her moles move closer together. "With . . . someone special. A young girl in a sweatshirt and leggings . . . one boot. I believe she needs some help. Will you please call me back?"

"Call back?" I ask Doryn.

"Voice mail. No one's there."

She finishes the call and puts her phone back in her purse. "Well, I left a message. I'm sure your friend will call back when she gets it."

Doryn hands me the book, and I take it. "What grade are you in?" he says. "Is it the same as Carter?"

Grade? I'm not sure what he means. "A," I say. I've heard it's the best. Wait, no, that's not right.

The mom stares. "Where do you live?" she asks.

And I wonder what she knows. What the library told Police.

The book is checked out to no one. The book is with me.

"Look." Doryn points.

The sky is dressed in pink and gold lights that fleck out over the ocean.

"West," I say. "The sun rises in the east. Sets in the west."

That's what the books said, but they never said it looked like this. All I saw were trees. I thought our tent meant west, and King's tent meant east. Now I remember. I've seen this sky before. But it might not remember me.

The mom steps closer. "Do you believe in angels?"

I look at her trinity forehead. "Ghosts."

She smiles. "Me, too. I'm sure your friend will be calling. In the meantime, do you have somewhere to stay—"

I shouldn't say it, but I do.

"Rain. My name is Rain."

16

"WE CAN TRY YOUR friend again in the morning," Kerry says as the big one, Carter, comes out of the bathroom. He's in a white tank top and pajama bottoms with cartoons. He folds his tanned, muscled arms casually and sits on the couch. His bed for the night.

How'd I get here?

My bed is as tall as in *The Princess and the Pea*. I'm going to need a ladder.

The walls have thin red stripes, peeled from a candy cane, on top of thick cream.

Carpet. I remember that one. My feet sink and leave footprints with their pressing. Takes a vacuum to wipe them.

Lots of drawers to hold lots of stuff.

A TV blares. I remember that, too. Doryn turned it to the loonies. Pictures with noise. The cat swings a hammer at a mouse. I should tell him the story about the tobacco man and the rat. But Doryn laughs, and I want him to keep laughing.

Doryn and the mom go to the bathroom to brush their teeth.

They're from California, Sacre-men-toe, sacred toes of men. Just visiting. They step lightly. The vacuum will take their marks away.

Why am I here?

She said we'd figure things out in the morning. *We.* Would there be a *we* if she'd found King? Or Jessiebel? Probably not.

In the morning, we'll talk. I'll tell her about me and the Winterfolk. She gave me a pink toothbrush cuz I didn't have one. She seems like the type of person who'd know what to do.

Carter adjusts on the couch as if it's uncomfortable. Three cushions' and six pillows' worth of uncomfortable. I wonder what his real bed is like. Ten pillows, maybe. His tank top hugs the muscles that saved me.

I keep my eyes on the TV.

She led me into this building. We went into a box called an elevator to lift us off the ground, and then she unlocked this room. Doryn and his mom will take one bed, and I'm going to sleep on the other. I think she knows I don't sleep on a bed like this.

Doryn and the mom come out of the bathroom at the

same time, both in pajamas. How does that happen? The mom carries a white robe.

She smiles. "The bathroom's all yours. You can take a shower if you'd like." She hands me the robe. "You can sleep in this."

It feels like a towel.

Doryn smiles, then sticks his eyes to the TV. He makes his way to the bed and climbs.

Carter fluffs a pillow and lays down his head. Locks of blond cover the green silk pillowcase. He smiles at me, too, and I smile back. I'd sleep on the couch, but they didn't ask me.

I go to the bathroom and close the door. It's bigger than the one at the laundry. The counter's made of polished rock with polished silver handles at the sink. Has both a bath-tub and a shower. But not better than my present from this morning. Nothing could be. I touch a piece of pink soap carved into a rose. I pick it up to smell, and sneeze.

I set the robe on the counter and turn on the shower with-out leaving a fingerprint. I'm expert at that.

The water is too cold. I turn it toward the red to get warmer and let it run so the noise gives me privacy. Then I remember to lock the door.

The toilet is too nice for me to do what I need to do, but that's what it's for, so I do it and try not to use too much of the paper. I press the handle and my waste disappears along with the smell. But I know it's not really gone. Just moved somewhere not so nice as here.

I take off Dad's sweatshirt, which smells of the sea. Then my tank, which sticks to me. My boot. And everything else. My locket stays.

The top half of me looks back in the mirror. Twice now I've seen myself like this. My skin is pinker than this morning, and glitters like my mermaid. The numbers on my arm are dark and thick. Permanent. If I had a phone, I could try Matisse again.

I rinse my underwear in the sink, hang it on a rack by some towels to dry.

The pocket is soggy. Full of sand. I smile when I find King's quarter. I get to the baggie. I pull out the baggie.

NO.

NO, NO, NO, NO, NO.

The baggie is empty.

Nearly empty.

A gap in the top closure. Water inside. A gummy white powder in the corners.

No.

I turn my pouch inside out. It wasn't sand I felt. Sand would be brown or tan. Not white, and not this fine.

I sniff the water.

Salt.

From when I fell in the ocean.

King grabbed at my pouch. He wanted to take claim of it, but I wouldn't let him. The bag must've opened.

I check the bathroom door to make sure it's locked, then throw my sweatshirt in the sink and check it again. Yes, it's locked. And the shower's still running.

My face in the mirror is red. I wipe my forehead. So hot.

I check the water in the shower. Hot. I turn it colder.

I go back to my sweatshirt and drain the water out of the baggie—pick at the remaining white grains in my pocket and put them in the baggie. Maybe they'll dry.

I drop my face in my hands.

I can't tell King. I know what would happen. He'll kill Cook. He really will this time. Or maybe King—

Two knocks on the door.

"Are you okay?" Kerry asks.

I wipe my nose. "Yes. I'll be just a minute."

She can't find out.

I put the baggie under the faucet and rinse. The white powder floats to the surface of the bag and surfs down a wave through the drain. I wipe my forehead again. Fill the bag up with water. Every bit of it. And squeeze.

When the bag looks as worthless as it now is, I ball it up and throw it in the trash. I take everything else out of my pocket and rinse them good, then the pocket itself. Last, I clean the sink.

I hang my sweatshirt to dry and jump in the cold shower to wash the ocean off my body. But not my hair. I need it in my hair for another day.

The stars shine from the window near my bed, but they're not as bright as when I see them from home, and I need them bright to make me better—make tomorrow better.

I'm careful not to wish.

I've been neglecting them.

I take care of the stars, and they take care of me.

The sleep breathing from the bed next to me is louder than Dad's. Doryn snores. Will Dad be watching out for the stars? Will he be looking for me? He was going to teach me the beads, but maybe he won't anymore. Not after this.

I wonder if King's looking.

My stomach is round and quiet from all the food, but my feet twitch and throb under the covers.

Carter breathes heavier than the rest of them, but he could wake any minute.

I pretend to sleep.

The mattress is soft.

King, you have no idea how soft. No idea what you were selling.

My body wants to sleep on this cloud, and I should let it. I'm so tired.

I should let it.

I don't need to make a wish to sleep.

The stars fade under my eyelids.

In this palace, there's not a single pea under my mattress.

17

MY BODY SLAMS AGAINST the ground. I gasp. A fish with no water, I open my eyes. Carpet against my cheek. And then I remember.

Carter stands over me in the dark, his hair too yellow to be that of a ghost. He whispers, "You fell. Like a rock."

I roll onto my back. The other bed hidden from me.

"Don't worry, you didn't wake my mom." He leans closer. "Who doesn't know how to eat with utensils or sleep in a bed, and why don't you talk much? Maybe you *are* a mermaid." He smiles. A nice smile. "You're kind of a beautiful curiosity."

I prop to my elbows.

He glances down from my neck.

I look where my robe's come loose and sit up to pull it across me. I want to get back to bed, but he holds his hands out for me to stay and I know they have the power to make me.

He slowly kneels, keeping his eyes heavy over mine.

His mouth opens. "I saved you," it says.

I scoot back.

But then his mouth is over mine. Covering. Wet. Smothering. Mint.

And I bite.

He jumps back and holds a finger to his lip. His eyes widen to see blood. "Why did you do that?"

"I'm not yours."

"I didn't say you were." He bites his own lip. "It's that guy, isn't it? The one who pushed you."

"I'm nobody's."

He presses his lips together. "Listen. I think you need help. Do you know him? The police said they've seen him before. They might know where he's staying, and it's not a safe place. Has he been keeping you or something? I've read things like that. My mom wants to help, too. Do you have a place? If not, I'm sure you can stay with us."

My fingernails are sharp for a reason.

His lips glisten. "You could stay with me."

A rustle sounds from the other bed, and Carter leaps back to the couch, where I can't see his face no more.

I climb back into bed, and pull the white sheet over me.

That didn't count as a kiss. Couldn't. I wipe my eyes and refuse to let it be.

My first.

I can't chance the phone. They'll hear me.

I wash my mouth and dress quiet—clothes still damp, one boot—and slip out the door.

The lamps in the lobby are dim, and the air is still. No one here except for me.

A lobby for ghosts.

The dark waits outside the front glass doors. Taunts. But I know better. I sit myself on a puffy couch embroidered with flowers, my book on my lap, and wait for the dark to lift.

I lean against a pillow, and my head tilts back. The ceiling is so tall I could fit my trees in here. A whole forest. But the light is artificial. They wouldn't like it. Their roots would strangle one another.

My head drops to the side, and I imagine how their limbs would scrape through the walls to search for the sky.

Telephone.

I sit up. There's a telephone on the wall.

It must be a trick. But the numbers throb on my arm and make me go to it.

The phone has two parts with a coil connecting them. I pick up the top part that has holes to listen and holes to speak.

The part attached to the wall has the buttons. I lift my sleeve and press the buttons in the right order.

It rings. One time . . . two times . . . three times . . . four . . .

"Hello?" says a voice pulled a long way from sleep.

"Matisse?"

"Hold on." The phone crackles loud, and I cup my ear. "Are you still there?" The voice is more alive. "Hello?"

"I'm here."

"Did you give it to him?" she asks. "He called me at work, and I told him you had it. You gave it to him, right?"

"You didn't get the message?"

"I had to shut off my phone, but I got the message. Um, who's Kerry?" Her voice is strained. "Where are you?"

My lips brush the phone. "They thought I was a mermaid cuz they pulled me from the ocean."

"A mermaid?"

"And I thought they were the three bears. But only at first."

"You didn't take any of that stuff, did you?" she asks. "Or anything else? Did someone give you something?"

I wipe my mouth. That kiss didn't count as giving. "No."

"Good." Her voice relaxes. "I'm sorry I didn't call her back. I didn't know who she was. You gave the bag to him, right?"

"I can't."

"Uh, yeah, you can," she says. "Don't be stupid."

"I told you. I fell in the ocean. Water got in the bag. It's all gone."

Silence.

"Matisse?" The coil wraps around my finger, and I watch it turn purple. "He didn't give us a chance to give it to him. He had a knife, and I fell in the water. I don't know where King is. I need your help."

"To help King," she says.

"Yes. And more."

The phone crackles.

"You wrote Winterfolk again," I say. "Why?"

"I don't know." She breathes into the phone. "Have you ever had a dream you thought was real?"

I've had many.

"Or experienced something you thought was a dream?" she asks.

Same answer.

"Is that what you are?" she asks. "Winterfolk? Is that what you call yourself?"

I squeeze the phone. "I live with the Winterfolk. In the Jungle."

She's quiet.

"It's our home." My throat closes. "But no one sees that. The city's gonna tear it down tomorrow. And now King is gone. It was my fault. He could be hurt—he could be . . . they'll all be . . ." I close my eyes and try to breathe. Pretend he's in front of me, telling me to breathe.

"Rain, where are you right now? Are you safe?"

I breathe.

"No one knows where I am." That should make me feel safe, but it doesn't. I look at the sign above the phone, and the words come to focus. "I'm at The Edgewater."

"Stay there. He might be at Lance's, who's another douche. I'll fix it. I promise. After, I'll pick you up."

"How will you fix it?"

"Trust me," she says.

I put the phone back together, and the coil lets go of my finger.

I wipe my eyes. I'm supposed to stay. While everyone's doing something except for me.

Where is King?

I grab my book and go to the front door. One push, and I'd be out in the dark—doing something. Maybe I could take the bus. We got here by bus. I could trace where we got off. I could find it like I found the stairs. But I'd need more light.

I look for the sun, but it's not ready for me yet.

I curl up in a chair behind a wall of plants.

The chair's arm tells me to rest awhile, so I lean into it and close my eyes.

Soft footsteps brush the marble floor.

I look through the plants. A young man stands behind the front desk in a coat and crooked tie. He has raccoon eyes. He yawns, which makes me yawn, too. He scratches his head. I must've made a sound, cuz he glances in my direction.

The elevator dings.

The door opens, and there she is. Kerry. I shrink into the chair.

She looks around the lobby in a white cotton robe. Same as the one I was wearing. She's looking for me. She is. But I can't let her see me. She'd take me back where Carter is, and it's not kind to talk about the past, but I would.

She goes to the desk, and the man straightens. They talk. He shakes his head. She looks around the lobby again. He gives her paper and a pen. She writes and gives it back to him. She looks around one last time before she returns to the elevator to be lifted away.

Once she's gone, I hear those soft footsteps again, only this time they're headed for me.

"Rain?" he asks.

I look up.

He gives me a folded note. The back of his hand is furry. I take the note, and he shrugs. "I wasn't sure if you wanted to talk to her." He scratches his head. Yawns again, then walks away.

I open the note. The mom's name, *Kerry*, with a phone number and a Sacramento address. And one more thing beneath the phone number:

I believe in you.

18

THE V IS WHERE I remembered.

A flutter of crows above startles me. They've perched themselves proud on the dancer's pointed toes, and judge me.

Well, I don't have much choice.

They say they're going to tattle, but I tell them I don't care.

They flap back at me.

Shoo!

The blanket mound's not here. Jessiebel must've done a good job last night to deserve sleeping on a couch.

Bob the ferret isn't at the window near the entrance either, so I try the door, but it's locked. Too early. Nothing appears to be open this early. I could keep walking. Now that I know where the sun rises and sets, I know home is southeast of here.

That way.

Not sure exactly. I massage my boot across the back of my other leg.

A loud click wakes me, and I look around for a gun getting ready, but all I see are people, and I remember where I am. I lift my head off the side of the building and shift to a not-so-numb part of my butt. Lots of people walking all directions. A tall man in a suit walks by with coffee, and the roasted smell floats down to me. My spoiled stomach gurgles, and I press it to my book.

The click sounds again. Through the entry to the V.

I lean around. Bob is at the window.

Do what King did to get money.

I go to the window and stand there some time before his head jerks up.

I find my voice. "Is Denise here?"

His head bobs. "What do you want with Denise?"

"I'm a friend of King's. He said to ask for her." I can't look him in the eyes when I say that untruth, but I hope I'm still convincing.

"A friend of King's, huh?"

I nod my head. For that I'm true.

"She might be up. I'll give you fifteen minutes, then you've got to be gone. This place isn't for kids. Go on. Go on in."

I shouldn't be happy to see a witch. I know they're not just in stories. But I'm a step closer to home. I open the door.

It's darker than it was in the hotel lobby. Wouldn't think it's day from in here, or that there's an ocean on the other side of the door, which I close behind me. The only lights are from the stripe of red around the rectangle ceiling and the stripes of blue around three circle stages. The center stage is the biggest, with a pole stuck through the center of a glowing blue V planted on the stage. The pole goes from the point of the V all the way up to the ceiling. The smaller stages are V-less. Long, high tables with chairs circling. Against one wall is another long, high table with chairs. The wall is covered with all shapes and colors of bottles and drinking glasses. The room's empty, but a door at the back shows a crack of light.

The blue V pulls me to center stage, and I climb the steps to meet it. We're the same height. I touch the pole at its center. It shocks my fingers. I let go and step back.

Drum music plays. Not real drums. But I can almost imagine myself home.

I look around, and the room's still empty.

I hug my book and spin once on my one stockinged foot. I close my eyes and spin around again. *Ba-boom*. And again. *Ba-boom*. And again. *Ba-boom*.

Clapping.

I open my eyes at the silk-robed witch. She smiles wide and clasps her hands.

My own hands tremble, and I press them to my hidden book.

"Lovely," she says. "Just lovely."

She climbs the steps and nears me.

"Are you my new *little chicken*?"

I hold my book tighter. Just yesterday I wouldn't have spoken to her. Now my mouth opens. "I'm no one's anything."

"Of course you're not. And you never should be. You have talent. A little rough, perhaps, but the elegance of a real dancer is there. Ready to make an appearance with proper training. The music takes you to another place, doesn't it? It does with me, too."

A jungle, maybe. Not my jungle. But one with rain forests and active volcanos that rain ash.

"I doubt you're aware how others could see you," she says. "So lovely." The eyes of a mother look me up and down, then stop at my boot. "Oh, dear. What happened to your other shoe, darling? What size are you?"

"I . . . I don't know."

"You look the perfect fit." She slips off her black, pointy heels with red ribbons at the back. "Here. Try these."

I've never worn ribbons. Especially not at my feet. "You think I could dance?"

Like King.

"Go on," she says. "Try it on."

I remove my foot from my boot and put on the dancing shoe. It fits snug, but not too much. I insert myself into the other, and wobble.

"Hold to the pole for balance," she says.

I grab to the pole with my free hand, but the world tilts. I drop my book and hold with both hands. *Steady . . . steady. Steady.*

How can she walk in these?

"That's right," she says, "the pole will keep you balanced. That's all you need. Find your balance. Try leaning away from it now, your body straight. Slowly. Yes. Majestically. Do you have a dress?"

"A dress?"

"What are you doing?" says a loud man's voice.

I collapse to the ground.

Bob is at the doorway, head quirked to one side. He's looking at her. Not me. "I asked what you're doing."

Denise smiles. Her teeth shine. "Oh, Bob. You interrupted us."

"She's a kid, Denise."

For a moment, color rises to her cheeks. She looks like she'll explode. But then she shakes back her hair and simpers. "We were playing. Don't be so serious."

He looks at me. "Is this what King sent you for?"

"King?" She looks sharply to me. A witch again. "She's hardly a kid if she knows King."

I shake off her shoes. What if King had walked in on me? What would he think? "I came to see if I could borrow some bus money. So I can go home."

"Bus money," he says. "You hear that, Denise? Bus money.

Come here. I need to talk to you."

She holds the pole to put on her shoes, and winks. "I'll be right back. We girls have a lot to talk about."

The ratty cover of my book glows blue and red. I don't think we have anything to talk about. She can keep her ribbons.

I grab my things and run to that doorway at the back with a sliver of yellow light. I need to find an exit. I open the door to a room of blue plush couches. All round are red drapes with gold trim.

Sprawled on one of the couches is Jessiebel in a silver sparkle tank top and black leather pants. Barefooted. His face is sand-dollar white.

I'm so glad to see him. I run over and kneel on his crumpled blanket. "Jessiebel, wake up." I tap his shoulder. "Jessiebel."

He doesn't move.

I pat his face with a small smack like I sometimes do Dad. "Jessiebel."

His eyes roll back, then flutter.

"Please wake up, Jessiebel."

His eyes grow wide and slowly focus on me.

What are you doing here? they ask. His mouth says, "Water."

Glasses litter the tables around us. I find one with clear liquid and smell. I think it's water. Water from a place like this. I put it to his lips, and he drinks.

"That's vodka," he says.

I move the cup away, but he grabs it along with my wrist and drinks down. "It works." He sits up and rubs his eyes. "I need to get out of here."

"I need you to help me get back home. But we can't go out the front. Is there another way?"

"There's a side door by the restroom." He stands and wobbles like I did wearing heels.

"Are you okay?" I ask.

"Of course he's okay." Denise walks in. "A little too much dancing. One too many beers. Right, Jess?"

He glares at her. "Sure."

She glares right back at him. "You leaving, little chicken? You know you owe me."

"You *owe* her?" I ask. "For what?"

He strips off his glitter top and throws it to the ground. Sweat glistens on his forehead. "I don't owe you for that."

She raises her eyebrows.

He unzips his pants.

"Stop." I cover my eyes. "You shouldn't owe her those pants. I think King wore them."

The witch chuckles. "You know King well, don't you, girl?"

"Naturally."

I'm dreaming. But I'm not. I know I'm not. I uncover my eyes.

King stands tall at the door. One eye—yellow-brown, less

swollen than yesterday. The other so deep I might swim in it. His hands hold my boot's lost companion.

"King." Denise backs up. "Your . . . uh . . . little friend was looking for you."

My arms are already around him. He holds to me, and I can feel the heat coming from his neck. He breathes hard, as if he's been running. His arms squeeze, and his hands reach to the back of my hair.

Jessiebel steps back.

King's voice is soft in my ear. "Are you mad?"

Yes.

I shake my head against him. No.

Now, more than ever, I want to be like snow, so I can melt into him.

He shivers. "Do you have it?" The bag with white powder.

"It's gone," I tell him. "The ocean took it."

He pulls back to look at me, and I confirm what he's thinking. His eyes glaze over. "Okay. We gotta hurry. Ready?" He squeezes my arm and doesn't let go.

I take the boot from him to join with the other.

"Great." Jessiebel's friend-face is gone. "I'm glad you found your . . . uh . . . friend. It's been a *rain* barrel of fun. Ha. Truly. I wish you the best in your journey. I don't know where I'm going, dears, but I'm not staying here." He turns to Denise. "Where's my kilt?"

King looks at me. "You know him?"

Denise tightens the sash around her robe. "Where it

belongs. In the dumpster. Along with that rag of a shirt."

"Those were my only clothes."

"Now you have new ones. You can thank me. You *should* thank me."

"And what about my shoes?"

"What do you think?" She turns around to face King. "I booked you for next week."

"You can't be serious," he says. "After you had her onstage? Bob told me. You know how I feel about that."

"*I* had her onstage?" She looks to me and laughs. "So innocent, aren't you?"

Of course not.

"What is she talking about?" King asks.

I look straight at him. "Nothing."

Denise stretches out a smile and looks at me. "I'll see you when you're ready." She looks to King. "And you and I are dancing next week." She softly nudges King's shoulder with her own, and King tightens his grip on my arm.

He adjusts his cap while she walks out of the room. "Let's go."

"Let's go." I hold my boots out to Jessiebel.

Who smiles wide and reaches to take them. "I wanted these."

King raises his eyebrows. "Who is he?"

"My friend Jessiebel. I have a friend."

"Yeah, she's my friend." Jessiebel is already putting on the boots.

King clears his throat. "Where's he gonna reside hisself?"

"In your tent." I untuck my book and hold it as a shield.

He lowers it to see my face. "This isn't a permanent situa-tion. And he's not bringing that glitter top."

"Don't be silly." Jessiebel picks up his blanket and throws it across his shoulders like a royal's cape. "I would never."

19

KING AND I HAVE taken the lead while Jessiebel trails behind. Our hands bump together with the occasional step for proof the other's there.

"What happened?" I ask. "Where is he?"

"He?" King tugs at his sleeves. He knows who I mean. "Disappeared."

"Disappeared how?" The way we can disappear, or the way my mother did? I won't know how to feel until I hear the answer.

"We gotta get home."

The tension in his words burrows into my stomach. Cook's not gone.

Jessiebel yawns behind us. King turns to look at him and grimaces.

"Maybe Matisse will find him," I say.

"Why would she do that?"

I tell him about the phone call.

"You trust her?" He shifts.

"Yes. She wants to help. I think she can."

His forehead wrinkles. "After we get to camp, I'll give her a call."

"I'll go with."

Our hands bump together again, and he holds on to mine. "You're not going anywhere."

Jessiebel catches up to us and wipes his forehead with his blanket. "Not going where?"

"None of your business," King says.

Jessiebel looks at me.

I let go of King's hand. Pretend his words don't bother me. Not going anywhere. No. I don't care.

Jessiebel rolls his eyes. "Fine, then can we get to wherever we're going so I can collapse? I'm hot as hell."

"Lose the blanket," King says.

Jessiebel tightens it around him. "No."

Two silver women with frowns pass us by—their eyes steady on Jessiebel.

"What he's *trying* to say," I tell him, "is you're half-exposed."

"Sweet Mary." He checks his fly. "I didn't mean to scare

those ladies. That's the thing with pants."

"No, I mean you're like half a ghost." I brush my fingers against the edge of his blanket. "Where we're going, we're supposed to be invisible."

"I don't do invisible."

I swallow my own arguments. "You have to if you want to be with us."

"Like I'm going to be less conspicuous shirtless? Did you see my abs?"

King slips out of his blazer and hands it for me to hold, then pulls off his sky-blue hoodie. My stomach flutters.

He gives his hoodie to Jessiebel.

I shouldn't look at King's body, but I'm worried he got hurt. That's what I tell myself. My eyes ripple over his earthen curves, so much harder than mine. Then he puts his blazer on and buttons it over his chest. He seems okay, but I'm still looking when he catches me. My cheeks grow warm.

I turn my attention to Jessiebel, who's pulled on the hoodie and rolls his blanket small and tidy before he tucks it under his arm.

We're headed south.

King and I walk farther apart.

I avoid the pebbles on the sidewalk as I avoid looking at King—along with the bits of broken glass and mysteries. My whole big toe's come out of my stocking. Another tear has started on the other. I'm sure I look a mess.

"My dad must be worried."

"He's fine," King mumbles. "After you went to that hotel, I went back. Told him what happened. Said you'd be safer there—for the night at least."

I stub my toe. "You were at the hotel?"

"You were at a hotel?" Jessiebel asks from behind. "What were you doing at a hotel?"

King pulls me along to get me to walk. This time with no tenderness. "What were you *not* doing there? When I got back, that family was getting in a cab, and you weren't with them. Ran all over trying to find you. Went down to the water, searched Pike. The last place I thought of was the V. Why did you leave?"

I yank my arm from him. "Why do you think?"

King spreads his fingers. "You didn't seem to be in a rush at that restaurant. And that hotel—"

"You were at the restaurant? That was you?"

"Didn't wanna disturb you." He checks Jessiebel, several paces behind. "You were eating."

"Disturb me?" My voice is loud, and I don't care. "Disturb me? I was looking for you. You think I wanted to be there?"

"In a hotel? A real bed? Away from all this? Yeah, why not? You were being taken care of. You were safe."

"Taken care of?" I hit him with my book. "I was taking care of myself." I cover my lips to keep the bad things from coming out of them, but the taste of mint slips through, and I wipe it with my fist.

His eyes turn to slits. "They were taking good care of you, right?"

I remember how I bit Carter, and my teeth dig into my lips.

He grabs my arm. "What did they do?"

I shrug him off. "Stop grabbing me. Like I said, I took care of myself. But you should not've left. Why'd you trust them? You trust no one. Even me."

"I saw you with their mom, and . . . just thought—" His eyes search around for the words, but he seems as confused as I am. Why did he trust them?

Unless he didn't care.

"You thought you could hand me off." My eyes sting. "That you were rid of me. Another birthday present."

His mouth drops open. "No."

"Then why?"

He breathes in and tucks his hands under his arms. "You deserve more." He lowers his head. "I thought it's what you wanted."

Why would he think that?

"And if I never saw you again?" I ask.

His eyes open with his truth.

He pushed me.

To let me go.

I walk ahead of him. Ahead of them both.

Jessiebel clears his throat. "That's not her world."

"Jess?" King asks.

"Jessiebel."

"Right. Jess. You ever been to the curiosity shop on the waterfront? The one with mummies, two-headed animals, and real shrunken heads?"

"A couple times."

"You ever see them Mexican jumping beans?"

"Uh-uh."

"They got 'em in tubes at the counter. Only they ain't beans, they're worms—not even worms—the larvae of a moth trapped in a seed. It jumps when it gets too hot so it'll roll somewhere safe in the shade. Gets too hot—dies. That store has them in tubes. Can't roll when they're in tubes. All they can do is jump. Makes them lose all kinda perspective. Imagine things."

I turn around to King. "Are you saying I'm larvae?"

Jessiebel nods his head while King shakes his.

"You're not larvae," King says.

"She's a bean," Jessiebel says.

"She's not a bean. Forget I said anything." King shifts his head from me, and now I'm thinking I look like a bean. A bean trapped in a tube on a counter in a store imagining things. Is that how he sees me? My world is a tube. Right. I turn around and walk again.

They murmur to each other, then pause.

Jessiebel breaks the silence. "I don't care if you're a bean. Or larvae. We all have issues. You like stories, right? You're still carrying that, uh, rag. Well, I have a story. Want to hear?

I swear there's not a single bean in it."

I shrug.

"I love a captive audience."

King glares at him.

"Not that you're captive in a tube," Jessiebel corrects. "Okay. Here it goes. One day, a baby was born to a great kingdom. The doctor looked at the baby and said, 'It's a boy.' The king and queen looked at the baby, and said, 'He has all his boy parts. How lovely. He'll be the perfect prince.' And they tucked him in a blanket. Only, he wasn't so very perfect. For instance, when he walked in the gardens he smelled the flowers too long, and as he walked, he hummed. 'He's touched in the head,' said the head gardener, and all the other gardeners agreed, because he was the head gardener. 'All he eats are noodles,' said the cook. 'Noodles curdle the brain.' 'He tosses his blanket on the floor. Every. Single. Day,' said the maid. 'I saw him playing with my gowns,' said the princess. The king picked up his rifle. 'If he doesn't like to hunt, how will he ever be king?'"

My feet stop so I can listen.

"The prince sought escape in the gardens. As he wandered, he came across a floating pane of glass. 'How curious,' he said, and he looked straight through. There, on the other side, was another boy from another kingdom. 'How perfect,' he said. The other boy smiled. They met their palms on the glass, and leaned in to kiss. Only, they didn't know the glass had been cursed with a thousand whispers. When their lips met, the glass shattered, slicing them open from head to toe. Out from their bodies came serpents. They wound their bodies around each other like garbage ties until they could no longer breathe." His arms entwine and lock together.

I hold my breath.

"The boy's parents ran to the garden. 'What should we do?' the queen cried. The king lifted his rifle and shot off their heads. 'For the mercy of us all,' he said. The bodies slithered away, and the heads were stuffed and hung as cloak hangers." His arms fall limp.

My fingers dent into the edges of my storybook. "That's the end of the story?"

He smiles. "What do you think?"

King takes his time as he looks at Jessiebel. "No."

I loosen my grip and breathe. "No more stories. I want to go home."

I look around at my giant map with a clear compass—the city, the sky, the streets. "Shouldn't we be going that way?" I point east to the steep hills.

King blinks away from Jessiebel at my direction. "We gotta go the long way. Through the Winterfolk. West."

"We can't. Not through them."

"Why not?"

"Hamlet."

"Hamlet?" Jessiebel squeaks. "My vote is with Rain."

King's brow furrows, and he looks curious at me. Wants to know how Jessiebel met Hamlet. What he missed.

But he doesn't need to know everything.

"Hamlet wanted you back home," he says, "and that's what we're doing. What's the problem?"

"No, he didn't. He tried to take me to a shelter."

King stretches his fingers. "He what?"

"We need to go the other way."

King takes off his cap. "I don't know what's up there."

Jessiebel turns himself in a circle like a spinning bottle. "If you don't decide, we're going to walk in whatever direction I stop. This is how I got to Seattle, and how I found you, my fellow weirdo and weirdette."

King grabs Jessiebel's shoulders and stops him. "This isn't a game. I bet Rain didn't tell you we're in a situation. You might not wanna stick around. We're leaving here. Tomorrow."

"Oh! Well, where to?"

King can't answer cuz he doesn't know.

But I don't want Jessiebel to leave, and I squeeze his hand so he knows as much.

"I'm staying," he says.

For a brief moment, the three of us are joined through Jessiebel. Until King lets go of him.

"Your choice." He looks at me. Still holding hands with Jessiebel. He knows I've changed—that I need to have a say. "You decide. East or west?"

I pull his hat from his fingers and twist my hair up into it. "Through Hamlet."

20

AS WE APPROACH TRAIN tracks, a loud bell dings and red lights blink. King's arm blocks my way at the same time a red-white-striped rail comes down in front of us. I cover my ears, but it doesn't stop the ringing or the sound of a train screeching toward. Vibrations pound their way through my feet. I back up to get away, but the vibrations still come. King keeps his arm in front of me, though there's no need. The train is loud all through my body. It's coming larger now. I've always heard it, but I've never felt it.

Air pushes at me the moment it comes. I tilt back like I'm a tree flexing in strong wind. King's long hair lifts like how I imagine a storm waves across an ocean, and it's so beautiful I can't look away.

The cars of the train pound past us fast. And we're still here. All of us. Two steps from finality. The cars still come.

Jessiebel throws his arms out to his sides and yells. Can't even hear him above the train. He motions for me to join. But I have no reason to scream.

Jessiebel smiles. Oh. It's for fun.

I make a sound. But it's not a scream. Jessiebel laughs and shows me again. His fists shake high in the air.

I look over at King, and he shrugs.

I close my eyes. And I scream. I try to make it for fun, but the train chugs and chugs and rips my throat open, and the fun turns to real.

And I scream.

For the tents that will be crushed, the Winterfolk scattered, Dad thinking about the next bottle, blond comb tracks, dancing hamsters, endless beads, and larvae stuck in tubes that can't roll away. For my Bruces and Evergreens. Mermaids who can't swim. My rocks. Locked wishes. And for the nothingness they all came from. For being pushed. Let go.

I scream.

The pounding comes and comes.

And I'm out of screams.

But the pounding still comes.

The train screeches.

I open my eyes, and King and Jessiebel are looking at me. Worried and serious. But then a train car passes:

WINTERFOLK

King turns to the train cars, and there are more of them. The rhythm of a drum speaks through the rhythm of the train.

And then they're gone.

The close-up pounding stops. The red lights turn off. And the rail goes up.

King stares off after the disappearing cars headed into the city of people.

"Winterfolk?" Jessiebel says.

King turns to me. "What did you do?"

I step up to the train tracks, metal bands over wood, and touch my big toe that's out of my stocking to the fresh run-over steel. It burns powerful. "You think people will see?"

He pulls at his cuffs. "It won't change nothing."

"But they'll see?"

"Who did it?" he asks.

But that's less important than the question of why. That's what he really wants to know but won't ask. Cuz the why is about whether we leave or stay.

I cross the tracks, and he follows. Doesn't ask more questions.

All around are squatty buildings in gray concrete and brick. The trains are long gone. And these parts are wordless.

"They look thirsty," I say. More thirsty than the rain could give.

"Supposed to," King says. His eyes are somewhere I can't see—a glance back to the city. "This is an industrial park."

Doesn't look like a park. No swings, and not many more trees than in the middle of the city. But these trees are young, not naturally grown. They line the streets in neat rows. Some cut by endless lines of power above us. Compared to the city, this place is deserted. No people except us, with hardly a car going by.

From a distance, freeways rush like flooded mountain streams, planes roar louder than a bird could ever sing, and that train still screeches high—metal on metal on metal, carrying a word.

We're close to home.

Jessiebel looks up. "Is that an eagle?"

And it is. A giant bird glides in a wide circle.

King snaps back to us. "There's a dump nearby. They go there like all the other birds. Doesn't matter he's an eagle." He glances at Jessiebel. "He still eats garbage."

Jessiebel turns to King. "People throw away the greatest things."

I walk between them. "No one lives here?"

"It's all factory stuff. Closed on weekends. See there?" King points. "That building's for holding frozen chicken. Those trucks bring them to sit in freezers until someone wants them. A whole building of frozen chickens. Thousands, probably."

Waiting. Frozen. Asleep forever.

"Over there, surrounded by barbed wire, is the state's evidence building. Anything police think they need to put someone away is in there—drugs, guns, blades, paper with names and fingerprints. Everything. All sitting there. Waiting to be used."

He nods south. "That way over there is a mail service, and the other way is another one. Packages going back and forth from all over the world. Anywhere you can imagine. What were those places you wanted to go? India, France, Italy? They come here. In these blocks of space."

I look around. But the buildings are still thirsty.

Jessiebel yawns. "Can we sit a minute? I need a break."

King's eyes stay on Jessiebel a bit too long. "She hasn't seen any of this, and her time's almost over. I don't care what you need."

Jessiebel holds up a hand. "What do you mean *her time*?"

King thumbs west. "Back that way is the biggest food store around. That's what I'm told. Got to have a card to get in and buy stuff. Like a library. But I hear you can't buy just one loaf a bread. Three of them stuck together in a bag. Can't separate. Everything in quantity."

"Hello?" Jessiebel says. "Are you going to answer me?"

I shake my head at Jessiebel. "Why's everything so big?"
I ask King.

"Maybe Jess can tell you. I'm sure he's been there."

Jessiebel stares at King. "Sure. Okay. Let's get this over
with. If you could buy a jar of peanut butter as large as your
head, would you?" He looks at me. "Would you?"

I think of our shoebox at home, the one my boots came
in. Now with one apple, two cans of tuna, and a loaf of white
outlet bread. Peanut butter would be good. "I'm not sure it
would fit in my box."

"Your box?" Jessiebel says. "Okay, never mind. That
doesn't matter. You could keep it outside."

"Well . . . then, yes. We could share it."

"Share?" Jessiebel asks. "That food isn't for sharing. Right,
King? I mean, who really likes to share anyway?"

King shrugs.

Jessiebel steps lively. "Yep, that food is for storing in pan-
tries, basements, behind false walls, under loose floorboards
and beds. For storing. Like everything else around here.
Waiting. Plenty to share, but it's not intended for sharing.
Most of it eventually gets thrown out. The Winterfolk—you
share with them?"

My breath catches. "I'm part of them."

King pushes Jessiebel into the empty road and dashes me a
harsh look. "No, you're not. Don't listen to him."

"What?" Jessiebel smiles. He lines up behind us. "That's what you want to know, right? What it's like to have enough?"

He and King lock eyes until Jessiebel breaks away. "How long have you lived here? Do you go to school? Study?"

"Shut up," King says.

My stockinged feet were black. Now gray. "I read, but I don't write." I look to King, but he ignores me.

"I could help you," Jessiebel says.

Jessiebel gets shoved into the street again. He holds up his hands, his smile gone.

"Stop pushing him," I say. Harsher than I meant. "You've had a lot of school, haven't you?" I ask Jessiebel.

"Almost graduated. I'm not exactly welcome back. Not there. But I'll test out. I'll do it when I'm settled." He looks at King. "Done pissing? How much farther do we have? I need to sleep, and maybe cry a little about my kilt."

King points at a trail that knifes through green hills.

My shoulders shiver on their own.

"There," he says. "The camp's through there."

And beyond the trail is the Winterfolk.

I replay freeing Hamlet's hamsters on the bus. "Hamlet's not going to be happy."

King shrugs stiff. "When is he?"

I peer through the blackness of the trail's end. "You think anyone's searching for us?"

King squints, too. "No. Look, there's Sabbath."

"Who's Sabbath?" Jessiebel asks.

"Heck's dog," I say. "He's good protection." Sabbath stands up between the trees and wags his tail. "He watches out."

"Still worried about the police?" Jessiebel asks.

I open my eyes wide at him. I did not want King to know about that.

Jessiebel mouths, *Sorry.*

Too late.

King cranks his head. "Police?"

I clear my throat and keep my hands steady. "What if someone saw my book? Like Police. And called the library?"

King reaches for my book, and I let him take it. He opens the cover. "What if?"

"Yeah, what if."

His eyes weigh on the library stamp. "Police saw this? Called the library?"

"When I was *rescued*. From the ocean."

King's lips seal together. I know he wants to say something. Maybe about whose fault this really is. But he won't.

"Would they know you?" I ask. "The library? Police?"

He shakes his head, but it's not convincing. He gives me the book. "We can't go back to the library."

I thought as much, but didn't believe it until he said it. No more books. "But we gotta return this. You said so. I'll do it this time."

"It's too risky. Might as well keep it."

"I'll do it," Jessiebel says. "They don't know me."

I cling to the book. It's mine.

"I'll find someplace else to get books," King says. "After we move."

"How long will that be?" I ask.

"Don't know, but we shouldn't be standing out here."

And we all know it.

He leads us across the road to the start of the dirt trail. That ends in my circle.

And that's when my feet stop working. Not numb or anything, they just won't *go*. Back to that circle. The beginning. I haven't done enough for people to see us. All I got were words on sidewalks and a blurring train.

"C'mon," King says.

I want to. "I can't."

King looks down at my torn and dirty leggings. "Hurt?"

I shake my head.

"Hey, Jess, give her the boots back."

"I don't want them back," I say.

Jessiebel puts the hoodie over his head. "She doesn't want them."

"Then what's wrong?"

"I dunno." Everything should be fine. Almost home. Dad waiting. Probably hand me a bag of beads. Take me all day to sort.

Maybe he'll still teach me the bracelets, and I'll pretend not to know.

I can wash the city out of my feet. Change out of these clothes—stiff with salt and the remains of seaweed. Eat an apple. Forget about MoonPie. Feed the hamster, if it's really there. Pack. See if King can find some thread. I still need to mend the tent. And we need water. We didn't get any supplies, and I'm thirsty. I gotta lot of things to be doing.

"You don't wanna go?" King says.

"I want to go." My feet don't. "Maybe we should get the laundry first. Half my things are in there."

"We already decided to go this way," he says.

"But we forgot the thread. And water. And toothpaste."

"I have some money left. I'll get it after we get to camp. When I call Matisse."

"Let me go with you," I chance again.

King stuffs his hands in the pockets of his blazer.

"Please don't tell me you keep her in chains," Jessiebel says.

King laughs his fake laugh—the one that dances in his throat, not his face. "We use thorny vines."

Jessiebel raises his eyebrows at me.

I can't look at him. Instead, I find words that were never my own. "For my protection."

The point of his mohawk has a sharp edge. "I think you need to convince yourself of that."

King glares, then turns and walks off the path. Examines the ground. He stoops down and picks up a rock. Turns it in his hands.

Jessiebel steps back. "Hey, I didn't mean anything. It's none of my business, anyway. Listen, I'm tired. All I want to do is sleep."

"Don't be stupid," I tell him.

I walk to King. My feet working now.

He shows me the rock—dark brown and oval. Nearly polished. "You ain't got one like that in your garden."

I nod. "Looks like a seed. Or a bean? Maybe I'll take it with me. Bury it. See what comes out."

"Naturally." He considers the rock. "Anything you want." His eyes chisel into the rock. Then they chisel into me.

He puts the rock to my ear, and I listen for it to tell me what it wants.

But all I hear is what King said. *Anything.* That's a full word. A filling word. I try to swallow it whole, but it's too much for me.

He lowers the rock from my ear.

"You don't have to go back," he says. "I mean it. We're supposed to leave today, anyway. I'll take you wherever you wanna go. Without Jess. Right now. You want to leave?"

My stomach tightens, and I can't look away from him.

"Rain," he whispers. He wants to tell me something. About him and me. But he won't. His eyes are pushing down everything he wants to say, and I know what's going to come out won't be enough.

So I don't let him.

"What do you have against Jessiebel?" I ask. "Can't you

see he's like us? I want to go home. I already told you. *Home*."
The word comes out, but I don't know he understands the meaning.

HOME.

Not the kind that will be gone tomorrow. The home that's meant to stay.

I wiggle my toes. I can't feel my words, but I can feel my toes. My big toe is strangling through the stocking, and I can't stand it no more.

I hand King my rock and my book.

"What are you doing?" he asks.

I double over and pull off my leggings. One leg at a time. The whole pair of leggings.

"That's not . . . ," he says.

My feet breathe.

I wad up the leggings and give those to him, too.

He hides them in his hand. "This isn't . . . ," he tries again.

I dig my toes in the moist earth and look at him. "You said *anything*."

He meets my eyes. "Yes."

"Then let's go home."

21

WINTERFOLK IN FALL IS worse than in winter, since cold preserves. Unwashed bodies and waste. Hits us before we reach the camp. It stings more than it stinks. You get used to it. I'm reminded of that when Jessiebel holds his blanket to his nose, the baby.

"Despite how tired my legs are," he says, "I really hope your camp is far from here."

I want to tell him how he didn't smell all that better yesterday before the witch made him clean himself. Instead, I hold my finger to my lips for him to hush. We're getting close, and my heart pumps fast. I push my rock inside one of the stocking legs and swing it loose at my side.

"Sweet Mary," whispers Jessiebel.

King looks behind at us.

I hold my weapon up for him to see.

What are you doing? he mouths.

I mouth back: *Taking care of myself.*

His long hair hangs in his face. "I'm going straight through," he says. "You two walk around. I'll meet you on the other side."

I shake my head, and he comes over to me. "You can put that down." His eyes move to the rock in my stocking. "If I go through the camp, I can distract, and you two can go on up."

"I'm not scared."

"Yeah." His lips lift in a smile. "I can tell." But then his head tips toward Jessiebel. "You know they don't take to newcomers. You got to look out for him."

I don't put down my rock. "Okay."

He straightens my cap to keep the cross straight, then turns his back. Walks away.

"Where are we supposed to go?" Jessiebel asks.

"Hmmm?"

King's nearly disappeared through the trees, and I almost can't catch him.

Jessiebel snaps his fingers in front of my face. "Where. Do. We. Go?"

"Follow me."

I fold my arms across my body, my book tucked in close and the rock down by my side. Jessiebel folds his arms the same. In front are branches, needles, and leaves, and all the spaces between them. You got to know the right spaces not to cause notice. I've lived in these spaces.

I duck my head to avoid the trees before they tug me with their arms and fingers to welcome me home. They don't mean harm, but I motion to Jessiebel to avoid them. He ducks the branches as rainwater does. Eluding. He's a trickster, too.

Soon, we see spots of blue plastic through the trees.

Jessiebel keeps his blanket to his nose. "How many tents are there?"

"Twelve, but more come in winter, like we do. There are other camps around, but I don't know them."

He rubs his nose. "Why do you join them?"

"The rain. You'll see. We're up where it's steep. The mud slides in wintertime, the ground's unsteady. I don't get out much in winter. Winter numbs—have you noticed—inside and out. Puts everything on hold."

He nods in understanding. "Winterfolk."

"You know what it's like now, don't you? That perfect moment. When you don't gotta worry about where to put your head or what to put in your stomach. To want to freeze that moment? Sleep like snow forever."

"But then you'd miss the spring."

My heels sink in a spot of loose soil.

Jessiebel nudges my arm and points through the trees. King's not walking straight through as he said. He's standing still. I move so I can see him better.

King and Hamlet.

"Why is he talking to Hamlet?" Jessiebel whispers.

I strain to see. "I don't know."

Leaves rustle behind, and I jerk my head. A squirrel comes out from a bush and scampers to the bottom of a nearby tree.

"Hey, there," I say.

Jessiebel turns to the squirrel.

"It's my friend," I tell Jessiebel.

Jessiebel nods, and I look back at the camp. There's more coming out from their tents. "See over there?" I tell him. "That tall, skinny guy with the long beard is Piper, cuz he got his windpipe broken one time being choked in his sleep. Scary, huh?"

Jessiebel points at my throat below where my gold beads hang. "Yeah, it's scary. But your windpipe isn't a bone. It can't be broken. It's the rings around it that probably got damaged."

"Well, then you go tell him his name shouldn't be Piper." I brush his hand away. "That woman in a red dress is Lady-in-Waiting."

"Who?"

"On the left. Away from all the others."

He searches and shakes his head. "I don't see her."

I point his hand to her. "There."

His eyes search again, then he turns to me.

"Stop it." I bump him with my shoulder. "That's not funny."

He presses his lips together. "What is she waiting for?"

"King would tell you to stop asking questions, but I want to know, too. To be saved, maybe."

"You see her a lot?" he asks.

Something skittles across my foot and I rub at it.

King points up the hill toward our camp and jabs his finger at it.

I hear him say my name.

"Do you?" Jessiebel asks.

"Be quiet. I can't hear what they're saying." Hamlet grows in height and steps closer to King. "Can you hear what they're saying?"

"I think King told him to stay away. Are they going to jump him?"

Hamlet leans his head down to King. Hunches his back. Rests his hands together in front of his chest like a rat.

"Of course not," I say.

At the farthest tent, someone else climbs out—young and dark.

"Who's that?" Jessiebel asks.

"Heck. King's friend. Remember Sabbath? He's over there. Look how sweet he is."

Jessiebel eyes Heck. "Yeah, he's sweet."

"I meant Sabbath—over there at his bowl."

"Maybe I should introduce myself."

"No, you shouldn't. Hamlet doesn't want to see me. I'm sure of it."

Heck pats King's shoulder, and the gesture is like a pause in the wind. Their bodies all relax.

Something catches King's eye in the fire pit. He bends down and picks up a yellow paper, then another, and another. All part burned.

"What are those?" Jessiebel asks.

"Our eviction notices," I whisper.

King drops them back in the pit, and his whole body sighs.

Piper and the others go back to their tents. Hamlet waves King off and heads off to his own. Just Heck and King are left. Not saying anything.

"Everything looks fine now," I say. "Let's go meet King where he said."

Jessiebel scans Heck again, and I pull his arm to tear him away.

I say good-bye to the squirrel, and we move through the spaces, not making a sound. Soon the Winterfolk camp is behind us.

We stop at the steep hill that leads to our tents. Now that we're close to home, I can't wait no more. My tent. My garden. My Bruces and Evergreens. Dad. "We might as well go up," I say.

"I thought we were supposed to wait for him here. I'm feeling a bit nauseous."

"It's just right up there." I point. "You'll feel better with fresh air. It's nicer up there."

"Okay."

We drop to all fours and start the climb. My weapon drags behind, and I hold my book snug to me. The sting in my nose fades.

I pause to catch my breath. "How long . . . how long have you been—"

"A conniving slut?" Jessiebel asks.

"Without family." I breathe hard. A tiny rock pricks my hand.

"A long time. A few months."

I laugh and rub my palm. "I should take back my boots."

"Hey, I hitched across three states to get here."

"Why here?"

"I told you. I spun myself, and this was as far as I could get from them. Plus, the weather's supposed to be mild."

"Sure. Wait until you're wet for nine months. I bet you didn't learn that in school." I look up to find my bearings. "We're almost there."

"Bless Mary, I hope so."

"We're on a flat part of the ridge up there. Our tents are green. You won't see them right away." I keep an eye out for anything moving that shouldn't be. "See those trees up there?"

"Way up there? You're kidding me. I think I'm going to . . ." Jessiebel holds his hand to his chest and heaves deep.

"Do you need water? Your face is pale."

"No. I just need to—" He crashes to his hands and retches without much of anything coming out.

I've seen Dad like that outside our tent when he thought I wasn't looking.

Jessiebel wipes his mouth and stands. He nods to me. I turn and keep going up.

"I need sleep," he says.

"Almost there." My bean rock bounces against the ground. Excited to be part of my garden.

"Where's your tent?"

"Above King's. Through the trees. Can't see it yet."

He sinks to the ground. "Too far." He presses his palms in his eye sockets. "My head is killing me."

I sit next to him and pet the feathery top of his mohawk.

"I'm trashed." He lays his head to his knees. "I just want to rest for a bit. Let me sleep. Here. This is fine. Wake me in a couple hours."

I pull at his arm. "We're almost there. We have water. I think. There's an ant crawling across your wrist." I show the ant where to walk so it hits Jessiebel's tickle spots, but it ignores me.

"Seriously. I don't care." Drool drips from the bottom corner of his mouth. "Sleep."

I slap his back. He doesn't move. Except for his nostrils, which open with each outtake of breath. I slip his rolled blanket from under his arm and tuck it under his neck. "Suit yourself. We'll be back."

Might be better anyway, so I can explain him to Dad.

I tuck my hair in my cap. Rub my sleeve across my face to clean off any dirt.

I slug against the earth. My feet plant themselves with each step, and I've got to pull them out again to tell them they're not home yet.

There. There is King's tent. And beyond.

Beyond.

I stand to full height.

Our tent is green. Hard to see. Hidden.

I walk around King's tent. My new rock taps against my knee.

My rock garden has been waiting. There it is. Calling to me.

Crying.

A circle with its guts ripped out.

My own guts rip.

My eyes play tricks.

Can't trust them. Can't listen to what they tell me.

My garden path surrounds:

Nothing.

I scuffle to the garden. A cloud of dry dirt rises and blinds. Me.

"Dad? Dad!"

My voice echoes.

"Dad!"

My soldier trees tower, my Bruces and Evergreens.

They look down. At me.

Me.

In the center of an empty circle.

Where our tent used to be.

2 2

"OPEN YOUR EYES."

I dig my fingernails in the earth. I'm on top of it, not under it. "King."

"Open your eyes."

I lose my grip of the earth and look up. His face blends in with the sun. "I didn't wish this," I tell him. "I didn't. How could he be gone if I didn't wish?"

He kneels down to me in the tree shadows. "You didn't do this. I should've brought you back yesterday. I never should've left." I feel his hand on my back. "Don't lie in the dirt."

"This is where we live."

"Not in the dirt."

A sound comes from behind. "What's going on? Where's her tent?" Jessiebel. He thought we were going home. I keep my face down.

Jessiebel doesn't say another thing.

"Get up," King says. "Rest in my tent."

I push myself to my knees and study the dirt—the castoff of rocks, the rot of trees, the carcasses of larvae. No glass beads anywhere.

I dent my palms in the dirt. "He wouldn't leave without me. Not like you did."

He covers my hands with his, and his fingers tremble.

"Maybe he didn't want you to come back," Jessiebel says from behind.

I turn around, and my hands leave King's.

Jessiebel hugs his blanket. "That's right. What if he didn't want you living out here anymore?"

"No. We've always been together. We're a pair, that's what he says. We're no good without the other." I have a thought. "Maybe he's found a new place for us. Getting our tent set up. We told him we had to leave, so maybe he got a head start."

King avoids looking at me.

Jessiebel kicks up some soil. "He should've left you the tent."

The trees above tell me. Given the choice, he would've.

"Maybe it was Cook," I say.

King looks up and across the hill. He stands. It's possible.

He believes. "I'll call Matisse."

I jump to take his hand, but he backs up before I grab it.

"No. You two stay out of sight. In my tent."

He takes my arm and lifts my sleeve. His finger rubs slow across the numbers, and they rise with my goose bumps. He clears his throat. Memorizes. Tugs down my sleeve. "I have some water in my tent, and another MoonPie. Eat it. You can change into one of my shirts. A big one. I'll be back. I promise."

He runs off before I know what to say.

Jessiebel steps toward me.

"Go eat the MoonPie," I tell him.

"You need it more than I do."

"He'll be back. They both will. My dad gave me a hamster for my birthday. He wouldn't've done that if he were gonna leave."

I scan the ground for the hamster, but there isn't anything moving.

"My hamster will be back, too," I say.

He dusts off the back of my shirt. "Okay."

I step away. "You don't think he's coming back."

"It doesn't matter what I think. What do you think?"

"That I don't have a home no more."

"That tent?" he asks.

I didn't always have a tent, but I always had a home. "No. My dad."

Jessiebel frowns. "You're still here."

My hands and feet look like mine, but they might as well belong to someone else.

"You're still here," he repeats, "and so am I."

He unrolls his blanket and wraps it around me. "I carry home with me."

I squeeze the soft fabric in my hands. "This?"

"For now. It takes me to tomorrow. What takes you?"

My eyes wander up the hill where King went, and I remember how his hands trembled on top of mine. But that's already in the past. I can't think about the past, and tomorrow doesn't exist yet. I don't know what to think.

Jessiebel taps my arm. "Where's that rock of yours?"

I lift the stocking off the ground, reach in, and pull out my new rock. Not picked by me.

"Where are you going to put it?" he asks.

I examine my rock garden—hardly a garden without the tent, but still mine. All those rocks. I'm the only one who hears their wants. I planted each of them.

"It's already fifteen wide," I say. I don't want to start on sixteen.

I turn the new rock in my hand.

And throw it down the hill.

23

I THOUGHT I'D BE hollow if King came back alone, but when he steps in the tent, I'm not. He came back.

His head casts down sorry. "I talked to Matisse. She's still looking for . . ."

"Cook," I say.

"Yeah. She thought I . . ." He laughs. Hoarse. And pulls at the back of his neck. "She thinks . . ."

"What?"

He shakes his head. "She was worried. About you. You were supposed to stay at the hotel. She went to the hotel to find you, but you weren't there. See? Even she wanted you to stay. I wasn't the only one."

"I didn't, cuz I was worried about you. I couldn't sit

there doing nothing."

He glances up. "I don't know where your dad is."

"That's okay. He'll be back."

Jessiebel and King exchange looks. But it's more than not believing me. King's not telling me something.

"Saw more Winterfolk writing," he says.

"You did?"

I know he said it to make me feel better, but he jabs the air with his elbows as he zips up the tent and hunches to a corner, where he drops a full plastic bag. I wish he was a storybook I could read. But he's not. He's the boy who brought the stories to me.

"You got groceries?" Normal words come out of my mouth. Expecting to turn everything back to normal. But they don't. "Your T-shirt looks like a dress on me. See?" It doesn't impress him. I don't know why it would.

He rifles in his duffel, throwing out shirts and jeans, then rips out a fleece blanket. He leans over to hand it to me. "You can use this tonight."

My fingers, clumsy as I take it, brush against his hand. His eyes flicker sharp on mine. Angry? The fast-dying sun shadows my face, and I'm grateful. I know I must be looking at him strange. I hide my mouth with the blanket.

He turns his head stiffly. "I'm going to unzip my sleeping bag and lay it flat. I think we'll all fit. I have a foam pad under here, so it should be comfortable." He pulls the zipper of his sleeper. "What've you guys been doing?"

I jump to the top of his bag to hold it steady while he unzips. My heart's the last to follow, so heavier than the rest of me. "Talking."

"Yeah?"

I fold down the corner of the sleeping bag to keep it taut. "So he understands."

"They can't just make you leave," Jessiebel says.

King shakes his head. "You're still talkin' from inside a house. Shut your door." He looks over at me. "You tell him anything else?"

"He knows what happened. What Cook did."

King stares at the ground a moment, then looks over at Jessiebel. "So we're good?"

Jessiebel's smile is thin. "We're good."

I stuff his scattered jeans and shirts back into his duffel. "We haven't had the MoonPie yet. We've been waiting for you."

He looks up at us. "That so?"

"We wanted to share it with you."

King tries a smile, but it doesn't complete. He runs his hands rough through his hair while Jessiebel and I spread the sleeping bag smooth. "I'll be back," he says.

Jessiebel turns to me with a blank face while King leaves the tent. It zips in one, hard tug.

"Where's he going?" Jessiebel asks.

A *TWHACK* startles me. Was wooden—tree against tree. Echoing.

Jessiebel backs into a corner.

"It's okay," I say.

THWACK!

My body locks in one position, anticipating.

The *thwack*s continue.

Jessiebel scoots over to me. "What's he doing?"

The words are tight in my mouth. "Storming. Un-upsetting himself. Though he shouldn't take it out on the trees. He knows he shouldn't."

"Does he do this often?"

"No." I reach over to Jessiebel and feel the top of his mohawk—just like a peacock's crown. "Sometimes he can't help it. He has a lot to be angry about—not finding my dad, sharing his tent, thinking he has to protect. He's the closest thing in the world to me, but I can't stop him when he's like this. I can take care of myself, though. He'll see. Plus, my dad will be back tomorrow and things will get better. Boys get angry like that, don't they?"

"What? Hit things? Erupt? Leave?"

"Yes. I don't ever do that. Not like that. Do you?"

"It's one of the reasons I'm here."

"Well, I stay quiet. You should try staying quiet."

And we do. Stay quiet.

Jessiebel and I stretch across the bag, testing what it'll be like to sleep all together.

"Do you always stay quiet?" he says.

"Yes. Well, most of the time."

"It kind of sucks," he says.

"Yes."

We listen to the pounding outside get slower and weaker.

My hands on my stomach rise up and down too fast. I try to get them to rest, but they don't. Not until the noise outside stops.

I close my eyes and hear the tent unzip. King climbs inside. Then a long, slow zip. His body lies down on the other side of me. His arm is bare against mine, jacket off from his rant. Hot and moist. His body worn.

I think of Carter's kiss. I don't know why, but I think of it, and how I bit him.

No, I don't always stay quiet when I'm angry.

My arm tingles against King's, and I move it closer.

King turns away.

"This isn't going to work," he says. "Jess, move to the middle."

I flatten myself to the ground as Jessiebel flips over me. And we all lie still together. Testing again.

And I feel alone, even though the three of us are side by side. I try to keep my mind inside the tent and not wandering up after those who have left.

I want to hold King.

But I think he might know that, and that it's something more I want—something smaller and bigger all the same— warm, wordless, and comforting. As warm as my face now for thinking. That's why he wants to stay away from me. He can hardly look at me.

I press my arms over my chest, and the rise and fall is slower now. So slow. But I hear him breathe slow, too, and it adds to my thinking.

"I can't sleep next to him," Jessiebel says. "Sweet Mary, save me."

"Then flip back over me," I say.

I catch King's eyes changing with his thoughts—turning inside to figure things out and then looking back out at me. His eyes settle a decision and split from me.

He rolls over to a space, his head at our feet. "Will this work?"

I press my big toe against his shoulder, and he swats it away. "If you wanna keep that toe, you'd better be careful," he says.

Almost like normal. Almost like it used to be.

"You want the MoonPie?" I ask.

Jessiebel climbs out of the tent with his cape. King climbs out with his radio. I'm the last to climb out with the pie.

I try to put on my normal self with normal thoughts and feelings, as if nothing has changed and I don't know anything about anyone. Maybe that will make King happy.

King turns on his radio, and hip-hop music comes through the static.

I open the pie. This one is chocolate. I try to break it in three equal pieces. Pieces are never equal, but I do my best and give myself the smallest.

"Do you see those stars?" I say before they get in their bites.

They both look up.

"See them shining on our food?" I hold mine up, and the milk chocolate illuminates. "This is star medicine. We eat this, and we'll see better in the morning." I pop mine in my mouth—the whole thing—and taste the sweet marshmallow, chocolate, and graham as it works its way down.

"I like that. Star medicine." Jessiebel pulls his apart and eats one side at a time, swaying to the music. "Do you want to know what I just wished?" he says.

I choke on the MoonPie. "You made a wish? On a star?" I check the sky to see if any are falling. Mom's star is heavier. "Was it that one?" I point. "That brightest one there?"

Jessiebel looks up. "Yeah, I think so."

"You've gotta take it back. Take back your wish."

"No," he says. "You can't tell someone to take back their wish. It doesn't work that way. Once it's out there, it's solid."

I open my mouth but can't say anything. He looks over at King, who takes a small bite of his MoonPie and lets it linger. Finally tasting something.

"Why should I take it back?" Jessiebel says. "Haven't you ever wished?"

"Yes, I have, but I'm not proud. Look how burdened she is. She's going to get sick on account of you. She's gonna give up, and then she won't be able to take care of us. Just look at her."

Jessiebel stops swaying. "What the . . . ?" His arms flap up and his cape billows behind. "If there's any medicine at all, it's *wishing*. If we don't wish . . ."

The rocks in my garden dull, and I rush over to them. "Don't worry, he doesn't know what he's saying." How will they ever shine again if we don't show them care? I rub my black-and-white-speckled rock.

"Do you hear this?" Jessiebel asks King. "Are you hearing what she's saying? What's wrong with you? Why don't you say something to her?"

After a minute, Jessiebel walks over to me. "Don't you want to know what I wished?"

"That's yours, personally."

The music gets loud to shame us for fighting.

"Come on, don't be upset," he says. "My wish wasn't personal. It was for us. The three of us."

I turn to him. No one's ever wished for me.

He wraps his blanket around his waist and curtsies to King.

I can't help laughing.

"Did you just laugh?" Jessiebel asks.

I shake my head.

"Actually," he says, "you giggled."

"I don't giggle," I say.

"You did. Didn't she, King?"

King nudges Jessiebel's toes off-balance, which only makes me laugh harder, and then King bursts into a laugh, too. A single laugh, but it's something.

Jessiebel throws his cape 'round his shoulders. "Forgive me." He bows to me and holds out his hand.

Before I can think too hard, I'm up and twirling to the music, and the stars twirl above us so I can't tell one from another.

King bobs his head to the music, and he moves his hips left and right and right and left. I spiral, and King catches me and we spin. I hold him tight and smell how sweet he is with MoonPie and soap with no lavender.

"I wish I had my kilt," Jessiebel says.

The song slows down now that we're all getting along again, the music not mad at us no more. And King's teaching me how to dance. His feet guide mine. His arms around my back. Around and around.

The trees turn to pillars; the leaves into tapestry; the dust beneath us to clouds. And I'm dancing in slippers, not the kind with red ribbons, but the glass ones with the size that fits only me. High heels. I dance on my tiptoes, and King is there for me to hold. Not some pole stuck in a V—cold and slippery—but warm and real. His head leans down to mine.

"Don't forget to brush your teeth," he says in my ear.

"What?"

He pauses. "I got you a toothbrush and some other things. And one for you." He nods to Jessiebel, then points to Jessiebel's head. "What is that?"

"My nun coif." He whips the blanket off his head.

"Coif?" King asks.

"Thanks for the toothbrush," Jessiebel says. "I . . . thanks."

I put my hand on my stomach. Lumpy now that we're no longer dancing and the pillars are back to trees. I tilt into the static of the radio.

"Are you okay?" King asks, and I know he's not asking about my stomach, but that's where I've shoved all my strange feelings. I just need to wait for the cramping and shrinking that always comes to take those feelings away.

"You're not my dad."

"I know I'm not," he says. "I just . . . Are you okay?"

I nod, though the sky is spinning. "I will be. Star medicine's always worked. She'll work again. You'll see. And when my dad comes home—"

"Rain . . ."

All I hear is static.

"He'll be here," I say. "I need to be patient like he says."

I pull King's skullcap off my head, and my hair rests around me. I want to feel like a girl with possibilities.

His face is blank, but he shuffles his feet.

I hand the cap out to him.

"You should keep it," he says. He turns off the radio and climbs in the tent. "I'll find myself another. Like you said. Soon, everything will be back to normal."

24

"RAIN, ARE YOU AWAKE?" Jessiebel's nose tickles against mine.

I push him away. "Yes." My eyelids are so dark that I know it's the middle of the night.

King breathes deep below us, and a high whistle ripples outside through the leaves.

"Do you hear that sound?"

"Tree wind."

His knees knock into mine. "Do you hear the twigs snapping? Can you hear it?"

I settle into the night and smile. "Night birds."

"Night hellions, you mean."

"You'll get used to it."

"How long did it take you?" he asks.

"I don't know. I can't remember." But that isn't true. "A long time. When I couldn't sleep, King would come in and tell stories."

"You've been friends a long time."

I rub my knuckles across my mouth. "Yes."

"How much older is he?"

"Two years."

"Two years can be a lot."

"A lot for what?" I ask.

King stirs.

Jessiebel tucks a strand into my recapped hair and speaks softer. "I had my first boyfriend when I was fifteen. It's normal to be feeling things. I've noticed."

I feel like the tent has opened up and bright lights shine on top of me. I turn my face to the pillow, even though I know it's still dark and he can't see. "Stop talking. I don't know what you mean."

He pats my head. "All normal. Nothing is wrong with you."

"He doesn't see me like that."

"He cares a hell of a lot about you. It's not hard to see. He'll be with you no matter what."

How can he know? Wishes change, and not even a star lasts forever. The world changes in our sleep, and sometimes when we wake up we have to start over.

"Please be quiet." I press the pillow to my eyes. "I want to sleep."

"I will. If you tell me a story."

"Fine." I speak into the pillow. "There were three little pigs—"

"Don't be lazy. Tell me one of *your* stories. Start with 'once upon a time.'"

"There was never 'once upon a time.'"

"There always is," he says.

"Not for me. Now shut up and go to sleep."

"*Shut up?* Are you still mad about the wish? I told you it was for the three of us."

"How could I be mad? I gave you my shoes."

"So it's the shoes? You should have them back. I want you to."

"I told you I'm not mad. Those shoes won't ever fit me. I'm grown."

"I'm glad you have it under control."

"Yes, I do. And I don't want the shoes."

"Great, I'll keep them, but they're not shoes, they're boots. Perfect with a kilt, if I still had it. You know where I got my kilt? *Once upon a time* I got a package from a boyfriend who was Scottish. Getting a package is a big deal, especially if it's a kilt from your boyfriend. And he loved me. He was actually from Scotland. I mean, he lived in Scotland. He *lives* in Scotland. I met him online. And we never actually met, but that's where I'm going to live someday."

"Online?"

"No, in Scotland. I *met* him online. On the computer—you

know, that device like a radio you use to talk to people and send pictures."

"Oh, I know what that is."

"Seriously, you need to go to school. He's the one who sent me the kilt. I never met him face-to-face, but *once upon a time* we could've. We so could've. And we will someday. He sent me pictures of him in his kilt, and OH MOTHER OF GOD."

"You loved him."

"I guess, yeah . . . What was that?"

"What?" I ask.

"The scratching on the tent."

"It was the grass. Maybe a rat. But rats are all knowing, you know?"

"ONCE UPON A TIME. ONCE UPON A TIME. ONCE UPON A TIME. ONCE UPON A TIME."

"Hush."

"HUSH?!" he says. "You tell me there MAY BE a rat clawing its way in, and you want me to hush? Do you know what kind of diseases they carry?"

"Hush, and I'll tell you a story."

"Yeah, I'll hush. ONCE UPON A TIME, ONCE UPON A TIME, ONCE UPON A TIME."

"Freaking hush!" King says. "Let her tell you a story."

The tent silences.

I curl my legs away from King. He's awake. I'd never be able to look at him again if he heard what Jessiebel was saying.

I try to explain. "I was telling him it's normal to feel scared with all the noises outside. I was going to tell him a story, but he wants a once-upon-a-time one. A real one."

"Then tell him," King says with an edge to his voice.

I reach back to find a memory, but I only see a castle with too high of walls. "I don't have one."

"You do," King says. "Everyone has a time. Everyone has a place. Including you. Tell him a story." His voice softens. "Once upon a time."

I peer into the castle.

25

NOT ONCE UPON A TIME.

ONCE.

There was a home.

With solid walls that never caved in and doors that swung open and closed. It had four panes of glass in front, four in back, and two on each side, called windows—so clear you might think their sole purpose was to dissolve the inside from the outside.

In that house, not a drop of water seeped.

A woman lived there. Tall with long, dark-brown hair. Each day she walked barefoot. Along a path of garden rocks that led from her front door to the ocean. She'd swim until the stars appeared, and ask her heart if it was ready to wish.

She wasn't selfish. She knew how the wishes of others burdened the stars. Made them sag and fall, then turn to rocks. That's why she'd only make one wish, and it would be perfect.

Each night she swam to the bottom and picked out a rock to give it her medicine. They'd never be as bright as stars again, but they still carried wishes. If she took care of them, they might come true. The stars above would see, and when it was her turn to wish, the stars would take care of her, as she'd taken care of them.

The path grew wider until there was enough room for the woman to walk beside a man, and together they polished those rocks out to the ocean. He didn't like how her heart looked to the stars. They were a pair, he'd tell her. And when she'd go out to swim, he'd go with her to remind her of the danger. Together, they'd collect more rocks to plant in her garden.

The path grew wider. There was enough room for a woman, a man, and a child, and the three of them would tend the dreams of strangers. The man watched the child fill buckets for her sandcastles while the woman swam, and he worried.

He worried so much he made his own wish. That the woman would stop looking.

The next night the woman swam, she didn't look for the stars. She kept facedown in the ocean.

The man and child waited with the sandcastle.

The sea churned, and a storm brewed.

The man told the child to stay. He swam into the ocean.

The child thought they must be lifting a very big rock if it needed both of them. The child walked into the ocean to help. She thought she could swim, but she couldn't. Instead, she woke in the man's arms by her castle. The tall walls had caved in, and the water had seeped.

No inside, no outside.

The child asked for the woman.

The man's watch ticked from one second to another counting the time since he last saw her. Never to look ahead again.

"An accident," he said.

But the child believed the woman had wished—and she looked for her in the water's foam.

The man gave the child a rock,

Black-and-white speckled,

The last rock he had pulled from the ocean.

The child looked inside,

Saw the wish of a ghost,

And planted it in her garden.

26

MY HANDS FIND MY locket in the dark of the tent.

"Your mom?" Jessiebel asks.

King rustles below us.

"It's a story," I say. "But not a once-upon-a-time one."

"As mine was." Jessiebel rolls closer and puts his arms around me. "Is that why you don't wish?"

"It's just a story." But my insides are caving like my sand-castle. "A stupid story about things that don't exist."

"If they're so stupid," he says, "why do we tell them?"

Jessiebel is asleep. King is asleep. I'm numb.

Which is far different from being asleep. Sleep offers dreams. Numbness is nothing. I move Jessiebel's hand off my arm and poke my toe against King's shoulder. This time I don't feel him. And he doesn't feel me.

Star medicine.

Makes you remember. Makes you forget.

I turn to the side of the tent and scratch it with my nails.

The tent scratches back.

I snap my hands to my body and scoot away an inch. Then three.

It scratches again. Two tiny scratches near the floor of the tent. Something presses against the plastic door—the shape of a small ball or a knee.

Scritch.

Or a rat.

I stick out my finger and touch gentle. The shape moves to the left. I wiggle my finger. The shape moves to the right. Rats aren't playful.

Scritch.

I stand quiet to the door and check Jessiebel and King are both asleep. And then I unzip.

The moonlight shines on Hamster 12, as black-and-white speckled as my first garden rock.

I climb out. "You found me."

His nose twitches.

I reach down to pet, but he skittles back.

"Oh, you wanna play."

His nose twitches again and something sparkles near his feet. Tiny as a pebble.

"What's that you have? Did you bring me some food?"

He backs up more as I pick it up. Glass, smooth and round. A bead.

"Where'd you get this?" I look for figures in the dark. In my garden. Behind a tree. Or at least one who might be trying to find me, not wanting to wake the others. But no one calls out.

I roll the bead in my palm. "Dad?"

Rain.

I'm not fooled. The wind carries my imagination.

The hamster scrambles back, and I step toward it. Then it runs and looks behind. Checking I'll follow. Which I do, of course, until I stop just to tease it. It runs back and forth to make me laugh until I take another step forward and it runs again. Down the hill and through the trees. My bare feet trample the sticks and dirt, but I don't feel it, they're still so numb. The hamster is fast, but so am I.

I catch my breath as he dashes around another tree, and I swing about—the bark rough and chipping in my hand. Nearly fall on my knees, but I pull myself up to see him scurry.

"Wait up!"

Down and down.

I go faster. Then stop when a figure steps through the shadows of branches. Not my imagination. Smaller than a man. Larger than a child. The shape of long hair.

The hamster runs to it.

The figure scoops up the hamster before it can get away. "Come here," it tells me. A woman's voice.

When I don't come, she moves toward me. Walks as if she floats.

Her hair is thick brown, but light as spiderwebs in a wind. She wears her red dress how Mom's hangers wore her empty ones.

The Lady.

It's been a while since she's spoken to me.

"Why are you out alone?" she says.

I look beyond, and my heart trips. The Winterfolk camp with its circle of blue tents and black garbage pit. I almost ran straight into them. My skin prickles. How could I lose track? I search for other Winterfolk, but the camp is silent as snow.

I don't think I even zipped our tent back up.

Perhaps I'm asleep.

I press the bead hard in my fingers, and the hurt is real. I hold it up to her.

"The hamster brought this to me. Do you know where he found it? It's a glass bead. One of my dad's."

She holds out her palm. "He brought it to you, did he? He talks to you like the squirrels do? Like I do? Let me see the bead."

I walk to her slowly, in case she'll disappear. She doesn't. She stretches out a hand of bones covered in flesh, and the bead drops in. "It's gold painted like my necklace. One of his originals."

She fingers the bead in one hand while she cuddles the hamster to her face with the other. "I recognize the workmanship." She looks to me. "But why do you seek?"

She breathes, and her breath covers me in emptiness.

"He's my dad."

"You're not a girl anymore," she says. "A young woman, it seems. Making your own decisions."

"I'm not. Not a real one. I haven't used the box."

King got it for me once, and I've never had no use. He explained quicker than I understood at first. I asked questions until he slowed and told me about the shedding and changing, as if telling one of his werewolf stories under full moon and all. I didn't believe him. But there were instructions inside for proof. Been a long time since I got that box of cotton. Now it's gone with everything else.

"Then maybe *becoming* one," she says. "Late, but not too late. A technicality. You don't eat enough." She clamps down her mouth as if her words left without permission.

"If I ate more, I'd be real?"

She rubs the hamster's belly. She looks to the sky, and her eyes brighten with stars. "Hold out your hands."

I do as she says, and she places the hamster back in them. Gentle. Its eyes watch me.

"Do you dream? All this time I've watched you. I wonder if you dream."

"When I'm asleep?"

"Not entirely," she says. "The best are those between

wake and sleep, when the impossible is possible. But here it can be hard to dream. Look above you. What do you see?"

I stretch my neck up. "Branches across night sky."

She follows my gaze. "Yes. Branches across night sky. Dreams should go up and out, explore and be seen, but they can't do that here. Ours get caught on all the branches. I tried. Do you see that one there, hanging in rags?"

All I see are leaves.

"That was my first dream," she says. "My biggest. Easy to get caught when they're big like that. They've gotten smaller to try and get through, but they still get caught—the bigger ones now part of the catching. You need a place to dream without obstructions. Where they'll be seen. You should try the ocean. Would you like me to show you?"

Her hair darkens. Moistens. Begins to drip.

I try to take a step back, but my feet are too heavy.

"That's okay," I say. "We're leaving tomorrow. King said we need to leave."

"You follow him like a little puppy, don't you?"

"King?" I shake my head. "He's my friend."

"Your friend?" She flips back a drenched lock, and it spatters my face. "You don't even know that boy."

"Yes, I do."

"Really?" The stars take refuge. "Did you know how he got here?"

I wipe my face.

"You don't know," she says. "I can tell by that dodo look

on your face you don't. A rat told me the story, because the story has many rats, and they like those kinds of stories. Plus, all stories are better with a talking rat, don't you think? He's fond of fire," she says. "Did you know that?"

"He's not. He never lights them."

I do know him better.

The Lady pauses and looks long at me. "You don't want to hear the story? About the fire, and how he got his blade?"

The hamster's wet nose rubs against my palm, and I shiver. "Stop it."

The bead drops from her hand. "I know how to find your star."

My body shakes. "You're not real. Everyone says so."

"I know a place. Where you will never be wet. You will never be cold."

"What did you say?"

She reaches for me.

Her fingers are the sea vines that strangle. Strong enough to pull me under. I rip from their stems, and the turning leaves of her dress blow away.

27

SPACES EMBRACE ME AS I run up the hill. I reach for the next space when the bushes ahead crackle. They break. And a body explodes from them.

I dig my heels in the soil. The impact hits me, and I fall to the earth soft to protect the hamster. And then my hat is off, and hands in my hair.

"Rain?"

I lift my face.

"God, Rain." King sits me up. "What the hell are you doing? What are you doing out here? The tent was open, and you were gone, and I didn't know what . . ."

I lean forward to catch his breath on my neck. I nuzzle against his shoulder. He's fresh from sleep, no shirt, his body warm against me. He was scared. That's how tight he's holding me. He shouldn't have to be scared. The emptiness won't take me.

His neck tenses. "What are you doing?"

"I don't know," I say, which is an untruth. He is real and alive. And here with me. "I'm sorry."

He hugs me hard. "Thought someone took you."

I want him to know he doesn't need to worry. My lips are near his neck, and I lean to set them against him. Just a small pressure on the side of his neck. Not even a kiss. And it's soft and salty as if he fell into the ocean with me. And then I do kiss, if that's what the pressure of a want is called. Possible. Not impossible.

I don't care what he did.

His hands reach to my shoulders and push me away. He's shaking me. No, it's my shoulders doing the shaking. "What are you doing?"

"I don't know," I say.

He leans his forehead to mine and takes a deep breath. "Oh, Rain." He taps my cupped hands. "What do you have there?"

I open my hands and the hamster peers out. "He found me." I close my eyes and rub my forehead against King's.

He leans back. A space between us, his mouth open with no words emerging.

"I'm older than you think," I say. "I've been kissed."

His eyes harden. "What do you mean you've been kissed?"

"When you left me at that hotel. I was kissed. I didn't want it, but there it is. I've been kissed, and I'm becoming."

He tenses his jaw. "Who did it?"

"That boy. Carter. He kissed me and his breath smelled like mint." King's would be sweeter—like MoonPie.

He scoots his feet under him. "I'm gonna kill him. What else did he do?"

"Nothing, and you don't need to kill him. I took care of it. I bit him."

"Bit him? And then what?"

I come up to my knees and lean in. "And then I became a werewolf. What do you think?"

He's not amused. "What happened?"

"Nothing. I went to the V."

"Your first kiss?" He grinds his teeth. "It was, wasn't it?"

"I don't think it should count as such if you don't want it."

"Naturally," he says.

"But I can't forget, either. I don't think that's what it should be like. I know what it should be like. I should want the kiss."

He stands. "We should head back."

I stand with him. "You need to replace it."

"What?" He's not listening.

"Yours is the one I want to remember."

"A kiss?" Now he's listening. He backs up.

"How old were you when you had your first?"

He breathes out hard. "That's a different matter."

"It is for boys, isn't it? They seem to have all the say."

"Not always."

"In my experiencing. He kissed me when I didn't want it, and you won't when I do."

"You're fifteen. And I'm—"

"I know what I am." I step forward. "And I know what you are. *I know you.* Will you do it?"

He fists the hat and hits it against his thigh. "Dammit, Rain." Takes another step back and examines me.

I know I must look a mess with my long hair gone wild and my dirty legs and feet. I pull the T-shirt down at the hem to make it more of a dress.

He steps forward and places his lips on top of my head. "There. Now you've had your second first kiss, you don't need no more."

My feet are warm against the cool ground. I tilt my chin up. "Let it be my first first."

He breathes in deep. I breathe in shallow. My heart races my breath. And that's all I am. Breath and heart. Heart and breath. The rest melts into the silver moonlit trunks of my Evergreens.

He lifts his finger to my bottom lip—and touches a parched ridge.

The trees whisper, *More. Ask for more.*

His eyes stay on my lips. "You need water."

"So do you."

"So do I." He touches his own lips, and I can't look away from them.

He drops his hand to my elbow and leans in.

His lips touch mine, and the trees sigh around us. His mouth parts, and his tongue brushes wet and light. Across my lips. All that I need. His hands move to the small of my back, and catch my hair in them. His fingers tug.

I pause, but then remind myself it's King and reach over his shoulders. My T-shirt rises, and he pushes me away from him.

"Rain," he says. Eyes like coal with blue around the edges. "Enough?"

No.

"For a first kiss?" His hands clench. "Is that enough?"

And because it's him, I nod.

He begins to walk. "We need to get you some clothes. You can't keep going around in my shirt like that. And some shoes. You need shoes. Why didn't you grab some of my socks? I don't know why he . . ."

I hate it when he turns like this. "Why what?"

"Nothing," he says.

I walk after him, and a twig snaps underfoot. "Say it. He? My dad? Why he took my stuff? Is that why you were storming today?"

"Somethin' like that."

"You don't need to take care of me. When my dad gets back—"

"He won't."

"Why do you say that?"

"Because it's true." He squeezes the hat in his hands. "And I think you know it is."

I hug the hamster to my chest. "Tell me what he said to you yesterday."

King picks a loose piece of bark from a tree. "It's not what he said. I saw it in his face. When I told him about you being safe."

"Was he drinking?"

"No." He bends the slice of bark in his fingers and matches it to one of the cross lines on the hat. "He was sober. I could tell he took it wrong. Was thinking you were somewhere better. I thought you were, too."

The hamster settles into one of my hands, and I press a finger into the peeled-tender part of the tree. "That's why he took everything, isn't it? He thought none of it was good enough."

He cracks the bark and drops it to the ground. "I should've told him you needed him. But I didn't. I left him that way. On purpose. Because you deserve more."

I rest my head on the tree, and a drop of water falls to my hand. Came from the tree. Not from me.

No. That's an untruth. It did come from me.

He tries to put the hat on me, but I push it away.

He holds up the hat. "None of what I have is good enough."

"Don't say that."

"Why not?" He pulls the hat on his own head. "It's true. You belong in one of them fairy tale books you like so much. I think you'd jump in if you could. Hell, I'd push you in."

"I don't want that."

"I'm not accusing. Your mind's been a whole lot better in them books than fixing on the things around you. How we live."

He starts to tear another piece of bark from the tree, and I press his hand down.

"You'll kill it," I say. "You taught me that."

His fingers brush against mine. Then he pulls his hand free. "Used to be—living here was like one of them books, and we were making it up day to day. Our own world. Working our way to a good ending."

The hamster wiggles in my hand. "We were."

"No. Cuz you never told me. I never heard until tonight. What your mom wished."

The hamster freezes. "I don't know what you mean."

"Yes, you do. That's what you said in your story. The one you told Jess. Your mom wished. What'd she wish?"

I hadn't realized he'd paid attention. "I don't know for sure. Only what I think. She wasn't there even when she was. And then she made it permanent."

He thumps the toe of his shoe on the tree. "Then I did hear you right. Her story, I mean. How come you never told me?"

I don't have an answer. I didn't know I had that story until this night.

He frowns. "Maybe Hamlet was right. You don't belong here."

His words, those words must be caught in the branches above us. They don't belong to him.

"I'm doing all kinds of stupid to keep us going," he says. "But you're . . ." He rubs his lips together as if he's smashing the words. "You called yourself Winterfolk."

I close my eyes. I hear him kick the tree.

"You don't belong here. And you don't belong with me," he says. "I was never meant to be your first kiss. You don't know me."

I open my eyes. "You mean the fire."

The wind blows his hair across his face. "How do you . . . You talk to squirrels and trees. The Lady."

"I'm not crazy."

He pulls his hair back to look at me. "I didn't say you are. I know you aren't." His hand digs into the bark. "She wants you to stay away from me."

"I won't."

"You should." The eyeshine is back in his eyes. "I convinced her—my sister. She didn't want to leave him at the house alone. Drunk like that. He was mad as hell I took his knife. Didn't know he'd fall asleep with that cigarette."

I swallow hard.

He picks at the bark again, and I slap his hand. "You're gonna kill it."

He rips it off and backs away. The leaves shield his face.

"You were only trying to protect."

He laughs. "You wanna know what Matisse said on the phone today when I went up the hill? Do you?"

I hold the hamster close to me.

"*Cook.*" The name is mucous as he spits it out. "He's dead."

"What?"

"I killed him. Yesterday morning. Like I thought I did. When I was getting back your boots."

"But I saw him. We both did. He chased us. That doesn't make any sense."

He backs up. Gets blurry.

"Ghosts," he says. "They're goddamn real, aren't they?" He takes another step away, and I don't see him no more.

"King?" The hamster struggles, and I drop it to the ground. "King!" I go after him.

I push through the branches, and those branches are so near looking to the Lady's vines. They scrape my arms and legs and snag at my feet, but I don't let them trip me.

"King!"

I stand still to listen. A movement to my left turns my head. "King?"

POP-POP!

The air ripples, and I crouch.

POP-POP-POP-POP!

Then silence.

28

THE CHILL OF THE earth presses into my knees. I know I need to move, but the stars are dim behind the thick night clouds, and danger hangs on the trees. No reasonable creature moves under such circumstances.

"King?" I whisper in the dark.

"Shhhh . . ." He emerges from my left and stoops next to me.

"Was that . . ."

"It came up that way from our camp. I need to get you out of here. We gotta go down."

He nudges my arm, but I push back.

"No," I say. "Jessiebel is up there. We can't leave him."

"I'm not. I need to get you safe first, and then I'll find

Jess. You can stay with Heck. I know him good. He's helped before."

"You mean you want me out of the way. Too bad there's no ocean here, or a storybook. Then you could push me into it."

He looks hard at me. "I'm not gonna argue with you. We don't have time."

"I agree we don't, so I'm going with you. You can't make me stay in some guy's tent while you find Jessiebel. You can't do that to me again. We need to go, right? So let's go."

He turns to the hill. "I wish I did have an ocean." Then he looks behind at me. "Well? Come on."

I scramble to him, keeping low as he does. We step light through the trees, and listen for sounds.

"Who you suppose it was?" I ask.

"Shhh."

I shut up only cuz I know he's right, but I can't stand the quiet. He holds up a branch for me to duck under, and then I hold it up for him. He knows his way along better than I do, so I follow close, wishing I still had my rock and stocking. I know he has his blade.

A commotion ahead stops us, and King tugs me down. It's the same mindless sound I probably made running after the hamster earlier.

He pulls out his knife and looks sidelong at me. "Get ready."

I don't know how to get ready. I scoot back and am frantic

for something on the ground I could use, but there's nothing bigger than pebbles and twigs. Two handfuls are better than none.

I wait as the rustle of leaves gets louder. I squeeze the pebbles. Ready.

The tree throws out a being, and my legs tense as King secures his thumb over the handle of the blade. The figure flaps near—in the likes of a white peacock, with a plume of tail feathers and a crown on top his head.

Jessiebel.

King stands.

I drop the pebbles. "Stop."

King doesn't hear. He rises with grace while the figure gets closer—turning from peacock to prince. King lifts his hand. Easy.

"Stop!" I jump in front of King. "It's Jessiebel!"

The white prince's arm raises with a glint of silver, a gun, and King's eyes dart quick to me. He can finally see. "Jess!" he says.

Jessiebel's eyes are wild as he waves the silver gun back and forth.

I jump up again. "Jessiebel! Stop!"

Almost on top of us, Jessiebel points the gun straight. Then his eyes go wide in recognition. "Run!" he shouts. "Fucking run!" He sprints past us. His cape catches the wind.

Before I can think, King grabs my hand and pulls me, and I find myself scrambling after them. Looking only ahead, not at any of the shadows that may be looming behind. Gate after gate of branches opens to us, and I will them to shut after we pass and turn into a fortress. *Grow!* I command. *Grow!* My fingers slip in King's, and I spring forward to hold them tight again.

"Turn right, Jess!" he calls out ahead.

We veer right, now on Jessiebel's heels. King reaches out and grabs one of Jessiebel's shoulders to hold him up. "This way!" We slip past him and Jessiebel follows us down. A steep part of the hill makes King's shoes slide, but I brace against his back and push him up before he falls. We fly down the rest of the hill, down through the blue tents, King now pulling because I can't keep all the way up, and we bound to the farthest one, where Sabbath sits alert in front of the tent. King cradles me down to the entrance and unzips. Jessiebel lands behind me. His hand on my back shakes while Sabbath licks my face.

"Heck! It's King, wake up. They're coming. Wake up."

"Who's coming?" I say.

"I told you he had friends, didn't I?"

A brown hand pokes out and unzips the tent the rest of the way, and we all fall in—me over King, and Jessiebel over the both of us, tangling our legs. We scramble apart into the spaces, and breathe heavy.

King snatches the gun from Jessiebel in the dark and turns it over in his hands. "Where'd you get this?"

Jessiebel breathes quick and heavy. "I was out looking for

you when these guys came to the tent, and there was a log, and I hit them with it, and one of them dropped the gun and I grabbed it and I started running and I heard them behind me, and Holy Mary, I started shooting and I don't know if I hit them or not. I just kept running. I knew I could out-run them if I kept going. I was cross-country—three years straight regional champ."

"Congratulations," a rough voice says. Heck turns a lantern on low. Green eyes light up, and I teeter back. "Sabbath told me something was up. How many are there?" he asks. He hunches over himself. The web tattoo on his neck pulses.

"Two." Jessiebel takes off his blanket. "And there's no need to be rude. I'm a fantastic runner."

"Sure," Heck says. "Nice track pants."

King opens the gun's cylinder. "No more bullets." He snaps it shut. "Did the other have a gun?"

"No, I don't think so. I didn't see it."

"What'd they look like?" King says. "One tall? Bald?"

"Yes. The other was in a dark hoodie. I didn't see his face. The bald one dropped the gun."

King and Heck look at each other with recognition. They know the guys.

I hug my arms.

Heck reaches under a pillow and pulls out something large and sharp. Above it, softly lit words blacken the side of his tent.

THE SPIRITS BIND OUR HANDS AND FEET
AND CUT OUT OUR TONGUES
BUT OUR EYES STAY OPEN TO WATCH THE HORROR
OF THE ONE WHO COMES.

Heck notices me reading. "The shit keeps coming, doesn't it? We don't have a choice."

I keep my head still.

"No one ever *asks* to die," he says, "unless the pain of being alive is worse than their fear of death. I've asked. Quiero morirme. It must be the same with being born. No one would ever ask unless they had to."

Cold air chills me from the door of the tent. I scoot myself into a corner and pull the T-shirt over my knees and tuck in my chin.

King glances at the words and shakes his head in a way meant only for me. *Not to worry*, he says. But I am to worry, and I can't believe King wanted to leave me alone with someone's demons.

King crawls to the open door and looks out.

Sabbath whimpers.

King nods to Heck. "You ready?"

Heck nods. "Keep your eyes open," he says to me. "Quiero morirme."

They step out together. King pops his head back in the tent. "Stay in here," he says. Then he closes it up, and Jessiebel and I are alone, and I'm reading those words again. I want to be outside.

"Heck is crazy," I say.

Jessiebel shudders with exaggeration. "Creepy." He smiles. "Who do you think it is? *The one who comes?*"

I feel numb. "Can't be Cook. He's dead."

His eyebrows raise. "Dead?"

"Yes."

"Well, good, I guess," Jessiebel says. "That's probably good."

I rub my eyes.

"Hey, did you hear Heck say I have nice legs?" He's changing the subject on purpose.

"He said you have nice track pants."

"I'm sure he meant legs." He stretches them in front of him. He's barefoot. "Where did you and King go before? You scared me to death when I woke up and couldn't find you. Well, not to death. Sorry, but you know what I mean."

"Why are you barefoot?"

"I wasn't expecting to be chased through the forest. My legs are sweating like crazy in this pleather, not to mention my butt crack. I wish I had my kilt. But I'm glad you and King weren't there. If I hadn't gone looking for you, I don't know what they would've done. Do you think—"

Sabbath barks.

"What's that?" I ask.

The foliage rustles on the outskirts of the camp, and

King's and Heck's footsteps move away from the tent.

"Oh, my King!" sings out a high-pitched, mocking voice. A drunk voice.

I grab for Jessiebel's hand.

"I know you're here, King! I can smell her ripeness through Heck's stink! Got a lot to protect, don't you?"

The rustling stops. They must be in the camp's clearing.

"I have her boots!" he says.

Shit, Jessiebel mouths.

I look over at him and try not to be accusing.

"Don't you want her boots? I know you do. You've shown you'd do anything for them. The boots do smell sweet, I gotta admit. Know plenty who'd like to try them."

Gliding steps take to the center. King's. "What you want, Lance?" His voice is heavy with control. "I know you're not here cuz of Cook."

"There you are. Yeah, now I can see you. You—under the stars. Kind of romantic. But you're hurting my feelings, man. Cook was my friend. Just like you were."

"Call that a friend?"

He laughs. "You've always been full of hell. I mean help. Always the one with a clean needle. I'm here for my Sabrina. She's gone and run off on me—silver, loud, makes fun noises. Thought she'd be here."

I point down at the gun King left in the tent.

"I'm feeling awfully empty without her," he says. "Kinda like you would, I guess, without these boots."

"What will you give me for it?" King asks.

"Just give us the gun!" a new voice shouts. Shrill. Scared.

"Shut up," Lance says. "Me and King are doing ourselves some negotiating here. I was thinking I'd give you these boots."

I crawl to the gun and pick it up. Jessiebel shakes his head at me.

"They're *boots*," King says. "What else will you give me?"

"Didn't you smell how sweet they are? Take a whiff. *Come*. I'm telling you, it's a bargain."

The metal of the gun is warm. Not cold like I thought it'd be. My hands are moist and getting slippery.

"Ah, Heck!" Lance says. "There you are. How you been? Keep your dog at bay if you don't want her to experience some of what you've had."

Sabbath growls outside.

"Stay," Heck commands.

"Ah, don't look at me like that, Heck. I know you've got mad love for our brother. It's cool. To each his own, I always say. Brother King's startin' himself a harem. Maybe *two-spirited*. Why ain't you smiling, King?"

I squeeze the gun.

"I'll give you the gun," King says. "But you need to leave her alone. She's had enough."

"Enough? She's a free agent, isn't she? Or is she yours?"

"She's nobody's," King growls.

I unzip the tent.

"What are you doing?" Jessiebel asks.

"Hand me the lantern," I say, and he gives it to me.

I step from the tent and hold up the lantern. The gun in my other hand. I squint at the two across from King.

"You *do* exist," the tall, bald one says. Must be Lance. The trees point him out as the lead. His clothes are clean. Expensive. He doesn't belong here.

The other one—in the hoodie and tiny eyes—could be a mole that lives in the dirt. He has silver rings on all his fingers. No. He doesn't belong here, either.

Lance smiles. "And here I was beginning to think Cook made you up. But he didn't exaggerate. No." He licks his bottom lip. "Not at all."

King turns to me, eyes full of anger. Used to be I'd rather die than have him look at me that way. But now.

I step forward, and Lance's face transforms in front of me. He's not Lance. He's Cook.

My breath catches.

"Don't," King says.

I blink, and Lance's face turns into his own again.

"I just want him to leave us alone."

"That's right," Lance says. "All I want is my gun and you can have your boots back."

I stop. "You have any bullets?"

"Ah, she's smart. No, I ain't got any bullets. See, I'll pull out all my pockets. Nothing in my jeans 'cept what's supposed to be there if you want to check. Creed, show her what you got. He's got less than I do."

The other guy pulls out his pockets and wiggles his fingers at Jessiebel, who climbs out of the tent.

Sabbath keeps his eyes on Heck. Waiting.

King walks over to me, and the lantern lights up his eyes. They burn. "Hand me the gun," he says. "I'll give it to him."

"If you don't mind," Lance says, "I'd like her to give it to me. In fact, I insist. You stay there, or deal's off." He motions to me. "Sweetie, come here."

King grabs my arm.

"Let me do this," I tell him.

He loosens his hand, and I give him the lantern.

I step forward again, and I keep taking steps until I'm several feet from him.

Lance looks me over. "You want your boots?" He holds them out and smiles. "Let me see that gun."

I hold it by its handle, the barrel pointed at him.

"Maybe I shoulda asked if *you* had any bullets," he says. "Do you like the feel of that gun? The power of my Sabrina?"

"There's no bullets in there," the other guy says. "I counted off the shots."

"I trust her," Lance says. "You trust me?"

I don't, but I stretch my arm out farther. King grunts from behind like it's *his* arm being stretched.

Lance takes a step forward, topples a little, and then holds out the boots some more. He reaches his other hand to the tip of the barrel and caresses it with his fingertips.

I reach over to the boots and touch the toes of them. Lance pulls them back a tad, and they escape me. He smiles and reaches them out again. I step forward and grab on hard to them. He doesn't let go, and I don't let go of the gun. Just a couple feet between us now, and I mind looking in his eyes but will never let him know. I stare hard.

"Let go of the boots," King says.

"Don't you worry. I'm just having some fun." Lance pulls the boots more toward him, but I don't let go, and I step a foot nearer.

"Let. Go." King's voice now louder.

"Now," Lance says. "The bag."

My voice trembles like my fingers on the trigger. "What bag?"

Lance smiles. "You like games, don't you? Cook told me it's you who has my bag."

He couldn't have told him. Not if he were dead.

"The bag is gone," King says. "If you don't believe me, talk to Matisse. Take your gun and go."

Then I remember what Matisse said. Cook called her at work. She talked to him. King couldn't have killed him when he got my boots.

"You killed him," I say to Lance. "Didn't you?"

Lance laughs and tugs on the gun, makes me lean into him. "He's not worth my energy. I think you know what I mean." He bends down, the tip of his lips and nose in my hair. He smells like beer and blackberries. I wobble. "Salty as the sea," he whispers. "Salty. And fresh. You, Rain. Are worth it."

King breaks loose.

Lance shoves me into King. The boots are in my hand, the gun is gone from the other, and I'm falling into King, who catches me as we go down. Sabbath barks as King's arms pin me down.

Lance laughs so hard he can hardly stand.

"Are you all done here?" a voice booms from the far corner. He can't be seen, but we all know it's Hamlet. Sabbath quiets down.

"Thanks for the help!" King's sarcasm calls out.

"Go on and leave now!" Hamlet says.

"Was just going to, sir!" Lance winks at me and stuffs the gun in the back of his pants. "Catch you later."

King stands. "If you cross over, I'll kill you. I mean it."

Lance backs away from us. Casual. "Oh, I believe you mean it. You do care so much, don't you?"

He smiles wide before they disappear.

29

I SMOOTH DOWN THE top of my hair, which I'm sure has something tangled and alive in it, and my throat dries with each step back up the hill.

Juicy blackberries. He smelled like my blackberries.

He can't. They're mine.

Just a ways more. I can make it. But my head swims in purple pinpricks, and his blackberry-beer breath follows.

I sway.

"Whoa." Jessiebel props me. "Hey, King."

He's by my side. "Hold on," King tells me. "Rest a minute."

Do they see my feet? I can't see my feet. I go to the ground, but not under. I'm not under. And then King lifts me, and I can fall asleep.

I curl atop the ground. Sprouts of weeds poke my cheek to wake me. I open my eyes to the night, but I'm not inside a tent. I'm under the stars.

The clouds have cleared. Shadows of Jessiebel and King move beneath Mom's star as they plant poles and stretch fabric. They're making a tent. *Re*making a tent. Jessiebel hums louder than the cussing from King, so I fix myself to the hum, but I'm so thirsty. My fingers dig into the soil. *Bring me water.* I dig, and the grit fills my nails. I keep digging.

"Hey." King holds my hand firmly. "What are you doing?"

"Getting water."

"Hold on." He leaves me, and I put my fingers to my mouth, but there's no water there. Only earth. I need the blackberries. They're mine.

I sit up. King's headed to the tent. I stand. Steady.

I walk through the trees. I don't need to see to follow this path. One foot after the other is the way to anywhere, and it's the way to my blackberries. King's sure footsteps follow, but I keep walking.

"Drink." He puts a plastic bottle in my hand.

I raise it to my mouth. A gulp and just one more. That's all there is, and not enough.

"They raided us," he says. "Must've been when they went back up. I should've followed them."

I give him back the bottle. "I need my blackberries." I need to know they're mine.

"You should sleep," he says.

I keep walking and stumble on something. I touch the ground to see what it is—a long, slender tube. Metal. The pipe we kept in our tent for protection. I pick it up.

"Let me see that," King says.

I hand it to him and keep walking.

I push the dark purple to the corners of my eyes. My stomach is small and empty, but I know how to fix it. As I always have. Not far now. Around the fallen great-grandma tree who nurses her saplings, and around her daughter who spreads long and reckless. To the wild bush with my own fruit as swollen as my tongue.

King is still behind me. Staring at the pipe. He throws it down and wipes his hands on his pants.

I adjust my eyes, because what's in front of me is wrong. The crossing is gone—I can't tell one side from the other.

The stars gloat.

They show me branches in hacked heaps on the ground, weeping pulp and juice from exposed, splintered ends.

My throat closes. I fall to my knees and stain myself in the broken bush. "What did they do to you?" I grasp her limbs.

"It's not your fault," King says. "You didn't do this." He doesn't sound surprised. He must've already seen.

I don't want this to be real, but the wetness on my palms and knees tells me it is and that I'm the cause. This was planned. You would need a hatchet for ruin like this.

"This is because of me." I reach for a small berry on a stem and squish it in my fingers. My stomach is not allowed to say anything.

"No," he says. "They wanna provoke, but I'm not gonna let it. I can't, and you can't either. It'll grow back. It's wild. Has strong roots. It's invasive. Nothing can keep it out, and it'll grow fast, you'll see. Everything grows here. And I'll get some food tomorrow. We'll eat tomorrow. I promise."

The stars hang heavy over me. I laugh. "Tomorrow always belongs to someone else. Not to me."

"If that's true," he says, "then you lied to me. You might as well be disappeared. You don't want nothing no more?"

I hold up a stripped branch. "This is what happens when I want. You were right. Nothing will make a difference."

"Then wanting's not enough." He licks his lips. Tentative. He looks up at the sky. "You've gotta wish."

My face stings as if he struck me. "You know I can't."

"You can. You gotta. Don't you dare disappear for real. Those stars are there for you, too." His hand stretches up to them. "Choose one."

Whispers.

From the sky.

I lift my head, and my eyes glide from one star to another. "I can't tell them apart." The stars are too many and too few. They'll fall as they spit out my wishes. Bring others down with them. "None of them are strong enough. I can't choose."

His hand drops. "You used to know."

The stars fade before my eyes. "Fairy tales."

"They didn't take your book. Do you want to read it? You can read like we used to. Maybe you'd remember."

All these dying stars.

Wink.

I open the cover. The first page is missing. And the second— torn from the middle. The third is there. Not enough light to read the words, but I know what it says. *Outside the castle there was a beautiful garden . . .*

"There was a beautiful garden," I tell them. A new story. "This one was guarded by a ring of thorns so thick they covered the sky."

"What's it guarding from?" Jessiebel asks.

My head hurts again. I lay it down against his shoulder. "The stars. They're full of poison."

King covers me with the blanket and takes the book. I don't care. He can have it.

My rocks are out there. Undisturbed. Guarding what's dead and buried—whispers from the past.

I wish. I wish.

She heard them, too.

My mother.

I roll onto my stomach and cover my ears. The rocks want me to tend to them, but I hate them. I really hate them.

I bring my hands to my face to smell the blackberries. Not even a ghost of a smell is left.

I wish.

30

I'VE BEEN HIT OVER the head. Most surely. I reach under my pillow for my pipe, but it's not there. At least I'm in my bed. My tent. I sink in comfort. I'm just hungry. That's why my head hurts. I know this hungry kind of hurt.

CRACK.

From outside. A green-tinted light invades my eyelids. I open one eye, and my head screams for me to stop, but my tent doesn't look right. I open the other eye. The blanket's not mine. Neither's the sleeping bag. I look around. None of it's mine. That's right. I don't have a tent. And I don't have my blackberries.

Another crack from outside.

"I got ya that time," King says.

"Yeah, but I have one more," Jessiebel says, "and I'm aiming for you."

I sit up. Which is a mistake, since my head might explode because of it. I spot a large bottle of orange juice next to the pillow. I twist and snap it open. I want to gulp, but I know to take a sip. The cool juice flows down my throat and through my chest. I wait until the chill is gone, and take another sip. Wait again, and then a big swallow.

CRACK.

"I hit you!" Jessiebel says. "That's two points now."

"No, it's one. Mine's closer."

"Let's measure," Jessiebel says.

I don't really care what they're doing, since a blueberry, sugar-sprinkled scone is sitting next to me on a clean white napkin. I twist the cap back on the orange juice and reach for the scone. The flesh of an already-busted blueberry glazes my tongue and eases my head. King was smart not to get blackberry.

His clothes are thrown in a corner. Such a mess. I wish I had my hand sweeper. I pick up his blazer with one hand and, between bites, fold it in a rectangle and stuff it in his duffel. I hold the scone in my mouth and pick up his jeans. I fluff them out in front of me to straighten out the legs.

A smear of rusty red shows across the front of the thighs.

Not from my blackberries, my weeping blackberries.

These stains are blood.

My brain rushes to last night. I don't remember anything

after the blackberries. But before—the blackberry-beer breath. And before that, I traded a gun for my boots. That guy—the one who smelled my hair—he thinks I have his bag. And before that? I touch my lips. Cracked, like King's.

"See?" King says. "Mine's closer. One point. I'm catching up. Better watch out. Let's go again. Grab your rocks."

Rocks?

I unzip the tent and climb out with the scone and King's pants. Jessiebel is in a kilt—the one I first saw him in—and he and King are gathering rocks off the ground. They look like *my* rocks.

"Where'd you get those?" I ask.

They both turn to me.

King straightens up and smooths his hair back. He touches his mouth briefly. He hasn't forgotten that kiss, either. "You're awake," he says. "How're you feeling?"

"Those rocks look like mine," I say. "From my garden."

King scuffles his foot on the ground. "Is it okay if we borrow them? We're not hurting them none, and we'll put 'em back. We're playing a game. Butchy."

"Bocce," Jessiebel says. "Do you want to play?"

I look to Jessiebel's kilt. Then to the scone in my hand, and back to Jessiebel's kilt.

"How'd he get his kilt back?" I ask King.

His eyes wander to the pants I hold in my hand. He tugs at the cuff of his long-sleeved shirt, and I take a big, nasty bite of the scone.

Jessiebel steps in. "*I know*. Can you believe she lied about trashing it? It's even dry-cleaned."

"What did you do?" I ask King.

He tosses a rock in the air and catches it. "We needed to eat. I promised we'd eat, remember? And now it's tomorrow—imagine that—and you're eating. I didn't leave you alone. Jess was here with you."

I take another big bite. It tastes of bile. "How did you get money?"

He tosses it again. "What do you think I did?"

"You tell me."

King tosses the rock again.

I want to throw the scone at him, but I want to eat it more.

"He didn't see Denise," Jessiebel says.

King rolls the rock in his hand. "No, I didn't see Denise. You really think I would?"

My face heats up. "I dunno."

"I got ahold of Bob. Told him how we have to leave today. He loaned me some. Said I could pay him later. He found the kilt in with the costumes."

I hold up the pants that show smears of blood. "Then what's with this?"

King and Jessiebel look at each other.

"I don't know," King says.

"They're your pants."

"It's from the pipe," Jessiebel says.

King turns the rock in his hand. "The metal pipe I picked up last night. Had blood on it. I don't know where it came from. He looks up at me.

I fold the pants in four.

He scuffles his foot on the ground and holds up the rock. "Do you wanna play? Jess taught me."

"Well, it's a modified version of the game," Jessiebel says. "The balls are usually the size of your hand, and they roll. And, of course, the court is a lot bigger, and it's flat. But this works fine."

The rocks aren't saying anything. "Okay."

"Pick out four rocks you can toss easily," Jessiebel says. "You usually play in teams of two, but there's three of us, and it really doesn't matter. We'll take turns."

I drop his pants inside the tent along with the scone, then pick out my rocks from the garden while they explain the rules of the game.

My black-white-speckled rock is the pallino—whosever rock gets the closest gets to score. I toss my gray-blue one with my eyes closed, and it lands farther than I'd expected. I must be getting strong.

"Good try," Jessiebel says. "My turn."

I stand next to King with a space between us. I feel every bit of that space like static electricity.

Jessiebel tosses his rock, and I turn my head from how it flies away. Instead, I watch his kilt move against his scraped and dirty knees. His rock lands about a foot from the pallino.

I turn to King. "Did you see anyone else while you were out?"

"No." He throws his rock wild, into a patch of weathered dandelions. Their gray puffs of hair scatter from the stems. "Your turn," he says.

I squeeze my brown rock with the black webbing. Feels good to squeeze it hard. I keep my eyes open this time and take aim. It lands behind Jessiebel's with a light thud.

"Nice," Jessiebel says. He glances at King while he positions himself. He tosses his rock, and it drops half a foot in front of the pallino. He twirls to us and smiles.

King aims his rock and throws. It soars through the air and thunks right next to the pallino. He looks at me. "I got enough money to get you some clothes before we go."

I rub my third rock, which is the color of moist dirt. "What about my clothes at the laundry?"

I have some jeans there, along with a flower shirt.

I still have things that are mine.

"Might be in the Lost and Found box, but we shouldn't go up there. Go. It's your turn."

"I don't want you spending on clothes. Not when I have some. If you give me money, I'll use it for that kitten we saw."

He laughs. "The answer's no. To your clothes and the cat. It's not worth going back up the hill, and we can't take a cat with us. It's your turn."

My finger rubs the rock harder. "They're my clothes."

"No."

I throw my rock, and it hits hard into King's, knocking it out of place. "You can't tell me *no*."

"No?" he asks. "Lance—he knew your name."

I swallow hard. "I don't care. We're leaving, aren't we? I'm going to get my clothes. And when I have money, I'll get that kitten. The bushes aren't there anymore to keep me from crossing. And I'm going to return that library book, too. It's not mine and I don't want it no more."

He walks toward my pallino. "I'll do it. I'll find your clothes and put the book in the drop box." He picks up the pallino, my speckled rock, and squeezes it.

His hands are so big they smother it.

"Stop doing things for me! I'll do it."

King drops the rock.

"It's not a good idea to go," Jessiebel says.

"I want what's mine. Give me my rocks."

"What?" King asks.

"My rocks. Give 'em to me." I go to my garden and plant the remaining rock that's in my hand. "They belong here, and you didn't have any right to take them for your game, banging them all up and everything as if they don't matter. As if nothing matters. Just cuz we're leaving, doesn't mean they're worthless. You probably scared the hamster away, too. Everyone doing things without even telling me. Put them back."

They both stare at me. I occupy myself with repositioning

my rocks so they fit just right again. As I work on it, Jessiebel comes over and places the rocks on the ground in a small pile, and then King comes with the rest of them and my pallino. I take them one by one and replant them around the empty circle.

If they wanted rocks so badly, they could've gotten them on their own. They didn't have to come and take those that already belonged. I lean over and brush the dirt off the tops with my fingers and wipe the excess across my bare, purple-stained knees. My locket hangs loose from my neck, wanting to take care of the rocks, too.

Jessiebel and King are still behind. Watching. But I don't feel close to either of them no more.

I lick my lips in search of leftover sugar from the scone, but it's gone. As is King's kiss. As is everything.

I reach for my locket. I lift the beaded necklace from my neck and lay it down on a flat rock.

I need to see her. The real her.

"What are you doing?" King asks.

I hold up my speckled egg and smash it down on the locket, but it doesn't do anything.

"Don't!" King grabs my arm as I go to smash it again.

I try and get my arm loose.

He clamps tighter to my arm, and his eyes flicker to the locket. "Please," he says, "don't."

"Let go of me."

He hesitates, but then his fingers open slowly. He steps

back and stares down at the closed locket as if it were dark magic.

My heart stops.

For just a moment.

I glance at Jessiebel, and his eyes are bright with excitement. I swing again at the clasp.

And again.

It pops open.

My arm goes limp, and I let go of the rock.

Inside the crackled glue edges is not a picture of my mom. It's me. In full color with wild brown hair and a beach behind me. I'm four or five maybe. No one here to tell me how old.

I look up at King.

"He said you look like her," he says.

I pick it up, expecting it to weigh different, but it doesn't. "I don't understand."

"You kept asking for her." He crouches next to me. "He didn't have any pictures left, but he had this locket. And I thought maybe . . ."

I rub at the hardened glue at the edges, but she doesn't appear. "This was your idea? You lied to me?"

His head snaps back. "It wasn't like that." He takes the necklace from my hand, and his fingertips brush my neck as he puts it on me. "It was hers."

I pull the necklace off and drop it to the ground. "I don't

want to wear a picture of myself. That's what I've been doing this whole time. When I thought . . . I thought she was watching over me. I can't believe you did that."

He picks it up and scrapes the glue off with his thumb. "Okay . . . okay." He puts it 'round his own neck. "I'll keep it, okay? Until you do want it. It was hers."

I try to picture her. To bring her back to me. But all I can see is a lady in a red dress. Who liked to talk of sleep and dreams.

Did I imagine her? Have I always? Is there another way I could've heard the story about King?

I shake my head.

Nothing's how it should be. I look to the day sky. Those stars are right to hide from me. Or else I'd wish on every single one of them, and I wouldn't stop wishing until they fell.

Jessiebel steps forward. "I'm sorry we moved your rocks."

"You're right," King says. "You should get your clothes. They're yours. And return the book. But I'll go with you."

"And me," Jessiebel says.

"After that," King says, "we'll pack up and go."

I stand, and my feet follow the rocks in my garden. The path is wide. Enough for three people to walk side by side. I won't be able to take the rocks with me. "Go?" I say. "Home?" It sounds wrong. That we must leave home to find it.

My garden started as a path, leading from the door and down the hill, until my dad found it. We moved the rocks into a circle around the tent.

The rocks are smooth beneath my feet. They show me where the door should be.

My trees look down and tell me. If it's not home now, it never was, and wherever I go next, I won't find it. I'm ashamed to look back at them. To tell them I'm leaving. For a place that is not waiting for me.

I pick up Mom's speckled rock, and listen.

What do you want? it asks.

My home is an empty circle.

I remove two stones from the shorter end. Where the door should be.

I whisper to all the things I cannot see.

"I want to go home."

31

WE STEP CAREFUL OVER the thorny blackberry branches. I clench my teeth to keep from talking to the blackberries upon blackberries, mostly fresh and waiting to rot, the rest smashed. They already know I'm sorry.

I hop to a bare spot of grass to wipe my feet.

Jessiebel jumps across to avoid them, but King walks through without disturbing any. "Come on," he says.

I follow, but can't stop looking back. All those berries. I wouldn't mind so much if they had been stolen away in buckets. My hands stiffen, and I extend my fingers to loosen them.

I press my thumb into my middle knuckle on the left and

it pops with a good hurt. King turns around, and I fold my hands together.

"My mom used to pop her knuckles," I say. "I remember that now."

When he walks again, I do the same on the right. Like she did.

He stops and lifts his head.

A skunky smell is near, but it's too sweet to be from a skunk. Someone's smoking pot. Had to keep in my tent when we smelled it coming from this side. My legs want to crouch to hide me, but I keep them up straight.

"Do you think it's them?" Jessiebel says in my ear.

I don't care. I swipe him away, and give King's back a little shove to get him going again.

The smell grows stronger. The source is around the tree.

A boy and girl sit on a big rock. The girl passes a joint to the boy. They don't belong here. Even I know that. His jeans have holes that don't look natural, and both have hair with straight-cut edges. They startle when they see us.

The boy stands and holds the joint out to King. The girl crosses her legs, and her short skirt rides up.

King shakes his head. At the joint.

The boy leans back against the rock, too stiff to be relaxed, and squints his eyes. He lifts the joint partway to his lips.

"What are you doing here?" King's voice is sharp.

"Hanging out," the boy says.

The girl looks at me the same way I do a bird I've never

seen—wondering what it's called and why it decided to visit. The boy looks at my legs, then down to my bare feet. King steps in front of me.

"You know what happens in these parts?" King asks.

The boy smiles.

King reaches into his pocket, and the smile disappears. "You know what would happen to the likes of her?" King asks.

The girl glances quick to me and jumps off the rock. The boy stands up tall.

King is taller. "This is our home. I suggest you go back to yours."

"Home?" I ask.

King turns to me. His eyes burn determined.

The boy looks about, and I try to see what he does. He's looking down at the paper trash and plastic bags.

I force my eyes up. To the trees. He should be looking at the trees, but he'll never see what we do.

The boy peers around King. To look at me. King jerks forward without moving his feet. He doesn't need to. They back up immediate, and the weeds and sticks trip them as they scramble from us.

"You think you should've said that to them?" Jessiebel asks.

"What?" Kings says. "Home?"

Jessiebel shrugs. "I thought it was a secret."

King looks away from us to the rock where they sat.

"Stupid." He kicks the dirt. "He left his sunglasses."

"I wish they left the joint," Jessiebel says, "but I'll take the glasses."

"Don't," King says. "It's bad luck to take anything not yours here."

"Like the blackberries?" I ask.

King's eyes search me, but I don't give him anything. "Don't hold on to that," he says. "You'll be giving 'em what they want."

"Did you mean what you said?" I ask. "This is home?"

He takes a deep breath. "I know every trail that leads here and out again. I've been here longer than anywhere else. I wanna stay. Like you do. But we can't. You see that now, don't you?"

"We could come back," I say.

"The police are going to be looking for me," he says. "Like Lance and them will be looking for you. It's not safe no more."

"But you didn't do it. It wasn't a ghost we saw. It was him. Matisse talked to him. She told me."

"You really think they'll care who did it?" he asks. "They're gonna be after someone."

Jessiebel puts his hand on my arm. "It won't be too bad to leave. We can go south. Camp on the beach. We'll have a fabulous water view. Better than my scare-ents. And in four years I'll cash out my trust fund, and we can build a house."

"But what about the Winterfolk?" I ask. "You know what's going to happen." I look to King. "Like Rosemary."

King beats his fist on his thigh. "I'm sorry, Rain." Then he turns away.

We climb again. The concrete wall up ahead.

When we get to it, King laces his fingers and holds out his hands for me to step in. I hand him the book, instead. Then I back up, as far as I can without slipping down the hill, and sprint to the wall, half jumping, half climbing. I scrape my chin as I reach. The tips of my fingers grasp the top. One hand slips, but I fling it forward and catch on again. My fingers are strong as steel, and I use my toes against the wall to get me the rest of the way up. I straddle the ledge and lie down on my stomach.

My arms hang to either side while I catch my breath. I focus on the book in King's hands to keep the world from spinning.

I reach out my hand. "Give it to me."

King shakes his head and gives me the book. "That's why you didn't wanna wear socks. So you could climb."

I sit up. The city is still there, along with the Space Needle. None of the structures glitter as they did before. A gull flies above, but I don't need it to tell me about the ocean.

King laces his hands for Jessiebel while I jump down to the other side. I expect to see Lance, or more of his friends, but the streets look as they did when King and I first came here. That was two days ago. I touch the scratch on my chin, and it stings just a bit. Seems longer than that.

Jessiebel hops down from the ledge and straightens out his

kilt. Then King. No one's around to notice us. Not yet. But soon we'll be noticed. We all know that.

I pull King's T-shirt down at the hem and brush back my hair with a hand.

"You look fine," King says.

My toes and toenails are dirt caked, my legs scraped, and my knees purple. I don't look fine.

"What do I look like?" I ask Jessiebel. "Do I look like a mermaid?"

Jessiebel covers his mouth. "No, honey."

"What do I look like?"

"Like you need a shower and clean clothes."

I look to King. "I want to take a shower."

"I thought you were gonna drop off the book while we get your clothes."

"No. I want to take a shower first. And change. If my clothes are still there."

The three of us take up the whole sidewalk as we walk. One or two people come our way, but they move to the curb to pass us.

We get to the laundry place with the *y* missing, and King points down at the sidewalk.

WINTERFOLK

"Still there," he says.

"It's permanent. It'll be here when everyone's gone."

"Nothing's permanent," he says.

No one's inside when we open the door. King takes me to the cardboard box with *Lost and Found* written in black marker. There, with a single red sock, is my full laundry bag.

I drop my book to open it. My jeans, my flower shirt, a sweater, four pairs of underwear, a towel, two pillowcases, and a blanket. All folded nicely. A note on top: *Matisse. Call me. It's important.*

I smell them. Lavender.

I hug the bag, and it crinkles. Something else in there. I pull out a yellow paper and drop it.

The notice.

King picks up the paper. "How'd she get this?"

"I don't know. I didn't tell her."

"Call her," Jessiebel says.

My stomach aches.

"I will. After I shower. I'll be quick. Will you stay here? Please? Don't leave me."

"We won't," King says.

Jessiebel wanders over to the vending machine.

"I mean it," I say. "No matter what happens, don't leave me."

The water runs warm over my stomach and soothes my swelling. I wish I had soap with me. I remember the bottle of liquid soap at the sink and hop out to get it. I rub some in my hair and let the water wash out the salt. Soon, the only smell left will be me.

I soap up my skin to get the blackberry stains off, and as I lean down to clean my feet, I notice a watery drop of blood on the inside of my leg. Brighter than the blood from King's pants. I check for scratches but don't see any. Another drop runs down the same route. And then I know.

It's not something I would ever ask for—like dying or being born—but it's here, and I'm here. I look around the room for something useful. I have a choice between a roll of tissue on the back of the toilet or rough paper towels from the dispenser. A metal container on the wall has two slots— one with a picture of a long, skinny thing and the other of the box like King once gave me. Each is twenty-five cents. Figures. That quarter King gave me is back in King's tent.

I wring out my hair and step from the shower, then grab some paper towels and pat myself down.

"King?" I ask from the door.

"Yeah?" Loud and clear.

"Do you have a quarter?"

"What for?"

My face heats up. "I need a box. They have them in here, and I need one. Now."

Silence.

A quarter slips under the door with the face of Washington, and he feels like a personal hero with that serious face. I insert it in the slot and turn the handle. The handle gets stuck, and I twist harder. I plead to Washington, and the box drops to the open drawer. I exhale. I don't have to look at the paper inside. I already know the instructions.

When I come out of the bathroom in my jeans that aren't so loose anymore and my flower shirt, I keep my eyes to the floor tiles. I don't want to see how they might be looking at me. King's shoes come into my floor space.

"I guess we need to go to the store?" he says.

"I guess."

Jessiebel smiles. "Better late than never."

"I'd settle for never." I place my hand below my stomach.

"Do you want some chocolate?" Jessiebel asks. "I saw some in the vending machine. I heard it helps."

I shrug my shoulders, but notice King going over that way and plunking in some money.

"It's probably why you were dizzy earlier," Jessiebel says.

"I don't want to talk about it."

King holds out a chocolate bar, which I take and put in my pocket.

"You should probably take some right now," he says.

"I'm not sick, and it isn't medicine."

"Well, I dunno," he says. "Do you want me to take you to a store?"

I nod. "Don't look at me, though."

"I'm not."

"I am," Jessiebel says, "and you don't look any different."

I hold my arms in front of me, and they're the same as always. I peek at King. He's turned away.

"You can look at me," I say.

King turns to me and nods. "You look like you," he says. Even if that's true, he doesn't look like himself. His face is as serious as Washington's.

32

I HARDLY REMEMBER WHAT it was like to be in a store. To have options. I'm in the aisle where King pointed me. I'm glad we're not in the larger grocery-store type. I'm not sure how I'd choose.

Jessiebel walks up the aisle. "You found the Bettys."

"The what?"

"Pads." He pulls out a box. "Here. This will work."

"How would you know?" I ask.

"I have an older sister, and it's not a big deal. Really. It doesn't make you a freak. You're Rain, and you'll always be Rain. Okay?" His eyebrows rise. Waiting.

I smile. "Okay. Is there another box that'll work? I want to choose."

"Sure. You probably want regular." He scans the shelves and pulls out a clear plastic bag with individual pink packages inside. "They're practically the same. Choose."

I choose the pink packages. "Have you talked to your sister? Since you left?"

"I have nothing to say to her."

"How do you know?"

He puts the box back and flicks it with his fingers. "I know."

"Hey!" King calls out from the other side of the store. "There's some flip-flops over here. Do you want some?"

I go to the aisle where there's a crate of different-colored shoes.

"Try them on," King says.

I pick up some green ones and put them on, but they're too small, then I try several more until I find some purple ones that fit fine. The thong part feels thick between my toes.

"I won't be able to walk far in these," I say.

"You don't gotta," he says. He shifts his feet and looks straight at me. "We don't need to go."

My arms prickle. "Why not? Aren't they gonna tear it down?"

A fluorescent light flickers over his head, and light and dark pass over him quick. "We'll see about that." The fixture stabilizes, and he's all light again.

I pick up another pair of thongs from the bin and pretend to examine them.

"I don't want to keep to the tent," I say.

"I'm not asking you to. I don't want you to."

"Then what are we going to do about—"

"We'll figure it out," he says.

And I believe him.

Jessiebel comes up behind him. "I found MoonPie. Want some?"

King and I answer at the same time. "Yes."

King digs in his jeans. "Saw a phone in back. Why don't you call Matisse while I ring up? Then we can go to the library." He dumps a handful of quarters in my hand.

"Don't leave without me," I say.

"Course not."

I find the phone. I put in two whole quarters and notice a word scrawled on the wall above the phone.

WINTERFOLK

I trace *Winterfolk* as the phone rings, and smile.

"Rain?" Matisse's voice.

"Hi."

"I need to see you," she says. "Where can I meet you?"

"Oh. Well. Okay. Hank's? Do you know Hank's Hot Dogs & Chili?"

"Yes, I can be there in twenty minutes. Is King with you?"

I'm not sure if I should say.

"Is he?" she asks.

"Yes."

"Good," she says. "I'll see you."

I hang up the phone and meet King and Jessiebel at the front door.

"What'd she say?" King asks.

"She wasn't there. Let's go to the library."

Maybe it's cuz of the changing. Or maybe the untruth. But my head buzzes. I couldn't tell him. He wouldn't trust her, and he wouldn't stay.

We pass Hank's Hot Dogs & Chili, and King asks if we're hungry.

"Yes." I try to keep my voice steady. "I'll drop off the book at the library and meet you back here."

King's eyes sag. "We're going with you."

"I thought you said you wouldn't keep me."

"I'm not," he says, "but you shouldn't be alone. I don't know where any of them are."

"It's right up the street. I'll be fine."

He looks up ahead to the library and then back at Hank's. He looks to Jessiebel, who nods at him. "You don't need to go in. Leave it in the drop box up front."

"Thanks." Maybe I should tell him about Matisse.

But Jessiebel winks at me as if I've won my independence and takes the laundry bag.

They watch as I head up the street, and my new shoes stumble me. When I get to the front of the library, I turn around to check if they're still watching. They're not.

I open the doors.

I didn't intend to go in. But leaving this book in the drop box would be a coward thing to do. The front cover is dirty with a crease through the mermaid's middle. The pages are warped and torn inside. Used to be strong as cloth. Not anymore. I take out the scrap of paper with the Sacramento phone number and put it in my pocket.

The same boy-shaped librarian is at her desk next to a tall stack of glossy books. She lifts one from the top and leafs through it, then passes the front cover under a machine-type thing that beeps.

I walk to the desk without letting my eyes wander to any shelves that are none of my business.

She knows I'm not a ghost. She looks right at me.

I set the book on the counter, and her eyes shoot down.

"I'm sorry," I say. "I didn't mean to get it damaged."

She picks it up and leafs through it the same way she did with her stack of brand-new ones. "This isn't checked out." She looks back at me, daring me to say different.

She knows.

"Borrowed."

She cocks her head.

"But you're right. Not checked out. You can fine me. I'll pay when I have money. How much do I owe?"

She pokes a frayed corner of the book into her chin. "I

can't fine you if it wasn't checked out."

I put both hands on the counter. "I'm responsible for it. Fine me."

She taps the book against her chin. "Do you have your library card with you?"

"No." My hands thump against the wood. "I don't have one."

She blinks.

"Do you live around here?"

I nod.

"Then let's get you one." She sets the book aside and pulls a form from a tray. "Here. You can fill this out." She holds out a pencil.

I press my thumb into my knuckle to crack it. *Pop.*

"I can't."

"I know you can read," she says. "Can you write?"

I crack my knuckles again.

A loose strand of bangs falls in her eyes, and she blows it away. She slides the form back to her and hunches over it. She writes. When she's done, she pushes it my way again.

"Fill out the rest," she says.

I look down. The middle of the form is filled out with an address and a phone number.

"That's not where I live," I say.

"I know. It's where *I* live. Now fill out the rest."

The words on the form blur, and my throat swells. I force my eyes to clear.

Name

I put the pencil in my fist, but nothing comes out.

Should be easy. I know my name. I know what it looks like.

Rain

But the pencil makes scratches that don't look like anything.

"Close your eyes," she says.

I look up at her, and she reminds me of King.

"Close your eyes and picture it."

I do.

I close my eyes. And picture my name.

Rain

I trace the first letter in my head. The pencil scrapes soft on the paper. When I'm done with the *R*, I start on the next, and then on to a full word.

A name.

I open my eyes.

Rain

She doesn't ask me for a last name.

She takes back the form and fills in the date—October 1. The day our home is to be demolished.

After she types into her computer, she hands me a plastic card. Hard, but flexible.

"What do I owe?" I ask.

"A dollar. After you pay, you can check out anything you'd like and take it home."

I squeeze the card.

"Or," she says, "you can read here. Anytime."

I let myself look around at the books, and I know there's more hidden behind those—one aisle ends where another begins. I don't know if she's serious.

The librarian smiles. "See you later, Rain."

I put the card in the front pocket of my jeans.

My head is still back at the library when a cop car startles me. I freeze while it drives by and then enters the station. I count eight cars in front, and at least ten police talking to one another and into their radios.

My stomach cramps, and I look for Jessiebel and King.

They're at a table in front of Hank's, across the street from the station. King watches the police as he eats. He sees them. I know he does. He shouldn't be sitting there. What is Matisse doing? Where is she? I shouldn't've told her where we were. I should've told King. My legs want to run, but I keep them calm to not draw attention. *Flip-flop, flip-flop.* My stomach tightens as I pass the station. *Flip-flop, flip-flop.*

King and Jessiebel look up.

"Sit down," King says. "Have some chili."

"Don't you think," I say, "maybe we shouldn't eat here?"

"Why not? Sit down."

I take the cup from him and pull off the lid.

He continues to stare at the police, and I don't know what he's thinking.

I try to drink the chili, but my body doesn't cooperate. The chili sits still in my mouth with no taste. From the corners of my eyes, I see another car arrive at the station.

"We should go home," Jessiebel says.

I nod my head and put the lid back on my chili.

"No," King says. He pushes the bag away from him and rests his head down in his clasped hands. "I'm gonna tell them."

A hole opens in my chest. "You can't do that. They'll take you. You didn't do it."

"I'm not sure. You didn't hear Matisse on the phone when she accused me. If I did it, then they *should* take me away. And I'll explain to them about you. I'll admit to it. I will. If they let you . . . and let the Winterfolk be."

The hole in my chest widens.

"King," Jessiebel says. "Don't."

"I'll tell them about Cook and Lance and everything," he says.

My fist hits the table. "No. That wasn't your fault. Why are you really doing this?"

He stands. "I couldn't keep you from getting hurt before, but maybe now I can."

"No." I shake my head. "You can't do this."

He steps back, and I stand up. "If you do this," I say, "I'm going to follow you in there. I'm gonna tell them how you watched over me. You've given me more than anyone else, and I won't let them think bad of you."

"You know I love you," he says. "Jessiebel, hold her."

Jessiebel stands and hugs me tight, his eyes squeezed shut.

"No!" I fight against him.

King backs away, and if my eyes are strong enough, they'll hold him here. I don't want him to leave. He *can't* leave. He'll take it all—my heart and breath.

"I wish!" I cry out. I scream. "King! I wish!"

He stops.

Across the street, a couple police turn their heads to us.

And then someone else hugs me, tight and feminine. Her hair, pulled in a ponytail, with purple tips.

Jessiebel's grip loosens.

"You're here," she says. "I'm so glad you're here."

Then she's hugging King. "I'm sorry. I didn't know."

My eyes let King go, and he backs out of her arms. Confused.

She breathes hard. Out of breath. "It wasn't you," she tells him. "It wasn't."

"What?" He shakes his head.

She pulls him over to us and hugs me again. Tighter. "I'm so sorry," she whispers.

My body shakes, and I push her away from me. She's in black pants and shirt, with matching black smudges around her violet eyes.

"What's going on?" I say.

"I had to show you in person." She pulls her large bag off her shoulder and hands it to me. "You have to see."

I don't want to open the bag. "What is it?"

"Winterfolk," she says. "It's all over the place. I started to

write it, and I told some of my friends. And, Rain. It's everywhere. And everyone wants to know."

"Everywhere?" King asks. Skeptical.

Matisse's face becomes serious. "Well, there's more."

Jessiebel puts his hand on my shoulder. "What's in the
bag?"

She looks to King and then to me. "Open it."

The bag blurs, and I sit on the bench. I open and reach
inside.

Beads.

Many, many circles of beads.

I pull one out of the bag.

A gold, beaded bracelet.

I rub my thumb over the fine-painted letters on the beads.

WINTERFOLK

I open the bag as wide as it will go.

Must be near a hundred.

"Where did you get this?" I ask.

She crouches next to me. "You recognize it, don't you?"
she says. "So, he *is* telling the truth. He's your dad."

Then she looks up at King. "You didn't do it," she says.
"The police confirmed that Cook was hit by a pipe. He died
of a contusion." She looks at me. "Your dad—he turned
himself in."

I squeeze the bag. "What?"

"Rain." She grabs my knees. "Cook went to your tent that night you called me. He was looking for you, and that's when it happened. With your dad. It's been all over the news. Your dad—he's been making these bracelets for you. He had a stack of notices and talked about the demolition. How the city wants to get rid of the Winterfolk." She shakes my knees. *"People do not like it.* That's why people are writing it. *Winterfolk."*

"He didn't leave me," I say.

King puts his hand on my shoulder.

Two police cars with red-and-blue lights turn on their sirens and speed out of the station.

"You've got to come with me," she says. "To the news station. They want to know who you are."

I shake my head. "You can tell them."

She laughs. "They want to see you."

The sun shines on the golden beads, and I squint up at it. That's when I find my star. The sun. It's big and strong enough to carry my wishes. To carry all of ours.

Star medicine.

Makes you remember. Makes you forget.

The beads sparkle, and I put the bracelet on my wrist.

A rustle sounds behind me, and I look.

A lady in a red dress.

Searching through Hank's dumpster.

Matisse shakes my knees again, and I turn to her. "I can't tell your story," she says. "It's yours."

I look back at the dumpster, but nothing is there.

"Will you come?" she says. "They'll have to let your dad go, right? Once you tell your story."

I look up at Jessiebel and King. "Can they come with us?"

She smiles. "Of course."

I hand a bracelet to Jessiebel and Matisse, then I give one to King.

He puts it on his wrist and pulls me up to stand. "This is good," he says. "Real good. Tell them about us."

"I'll tell them about Hamlet's drums," I say. "And the dancing hamsters."

King nods. "The squirrels, and the rats."

"And Sabbath," Jessiebel says, "and the one who comes."

Matisse picks up her bag. "About the Winterfolk."

"And home," King says.

"Home."

Where my Bruces and Evergreens cover the sky in their branches, and leave room for us to dream.

33

THE MORNING LIGHT IS tinted green. The cries of gulls sound above. They want to tell me about the ocean. But now I remember. About the night she walked into it and never came home.

Sometimes I still pretend I'm a ghost.

My kitten purrs at my belly, and I don't pretend anymore. I reach under my pillow until I feel the solid cover of my book and pull it out. A notebook full of practice letters. As and Bs. And so on to Zs.

Today is the day. I turn to a clean page, and I write.

WINTERFOLK

ACKNOWLEDGMENTS

I always read the acknowledgments at the end of a book, because it reminds me how a community is required to get a story published, and that I'll never be left on my own to complete such a task. *Winterfolk* is no exception.

First, I want to thank the Hamline community—Anne Ursu, for seeing a dream and showing me reality; Laura Ruby, for asking the questions that revealed the story's heart; Jane Resh Thomas, Marsha Qualey, Kelly Easton, Claire Rudolf Murphy, and Gene Luen Yang, who read the first pages and gave me words of confidence that I would lean on throughout the writing process; Phyllis Root, who cheered and pushed me; Swati Avasthi, Jacqueline Briggs Martin, Emily Jenkins, Ron Koertge, Gary D. Schmidt, and Marsha

Wilson Chall, whose lectures and workshops inspired me; my talented workshop buddies, who said all the right things; and my team of Hamsters—Andrew John, Eddy Giorgi, Elizabeth Aldridge, Kate Fitzgerald, Kristi Romo, Leah Hilsabeck-Lowrey, Meg Cannistra, Nikki Ericksen, Nina Bricko, Randy Bonser, Sarah Marie Eschweiler, and Sean Tulien—my strong partners in this writing dance.

I want to thank my agent, Beth Phelan at the Bent Agency, for seeing the potential in the story and taking a chance. It was with her instinct and care that this story became a book. I also want to thank my editor, Tara Weikum, for that beautiful word *yes* and challenging me to dig deeper and reach farther than I thought possible.

Thank you to the readers, editors, and copy editors at HarperCollins who constantly astounded me with their attention to detail. Also, a big thank-you to Sarah Nichole Kaufman, for designing the jacket of *Winterfolk*, and to Matt Saunders, the artist, who captured the solitude and solace of *Winterfolk* to perfection.

I was fortunate enough to receive strong encouragement about my writing at a young age from teachers, family, and friends. Thank you, Mom and Dad, Laurie, Melissa, Mike, Amanda, Missy, Daphne, and Soudie. Thank you, Nana, for passing on your love for reading, as well as your romance collection, and Grandma Kolby for passing on your love of words and talent in poetry.

Thank you to my husband, James, and my son, Bodi, for

your endless hugs and bottomless patience. Thank you for loving and accepting this woman whose mind is always half-way in a story. I hope what's left is enough.

Finally, thank you to the Eastside residents of Tent City 4. You answered my questions with open hearts and minds and taught me the difference between a shelter and a community.